Kellie's Dreams

By

Johanna Jackson

Romance and Spiritual Intrigue

New Generation Publishing

Dedicated to my husband Anthony and our wonderful family and friends

Acknowledgements

My first thanks must go to my existing readers, for the fact that they took a risk on buying a book from a new author. Thank you so much for supporting my first and now my second endeavour. I truly hope your lovely reviews continue and that you find as much pleasure, if not more, in reading this new story of love and spirituality; in case you are wondering, yes, there is a cheeky bit of raunchiness thrown in.

My second thanks go to my ever-supportive husband, family and friends, along with my enthusiastic reviewers of the early drafts of this new story. You have all helped me with your honest opinions and positive inputs. The truth is, I continue to grow as an author through your feedback and I truly appreciate all of your support, more than you probably know. Thank you!

Finally, thanks go again to New Generation Publishing for their help and encouragement, which keeps me positive and focused.

Contents

Part 1

Chapter 1

Dreams

Voices were seeping through the haze of her mind as Kellie was reluctantly dragged into the reality of daytime. Out of what had felt like the depths of sleep, one voice from this dream seemed stronger than the others. From what Kellie could recall, the voice had been speaking to her in broken English. The words didn't flow like any normal language would and the voice seemed to have an old feel to it, but somehow – and she didn't know quite how – although it had been a dream, Kellie still remembered the spoken words.

"I chose to go early. I knew I had to, to save you. I know it doesn't make sense now, but it will one day soon and you will know. You will realise that it was all meant to be and will be repeated. You will lose him, but he will die proud and protecting you, as I did all those years ago. Love him, it will never leave him. He will return stronger, different and more able to provide for you and cherish you, as he does now."

The words almost seemed like a prayer and feeling slightly disturbed that it had happened again, Kellie felt like her mind was being taken over by these strange dreams. What did they mean? It was beginning to really bother her that for several weeks now, these dreams had invaded her sleep, quite often leaving her feeling agitated on waking. Tom had said they were premonitions, but that was just him being a fantasist. At least that's what Kellie had convinced herself of, but maybe Tom had a point and maybe they *were* some kind of premonition. Was that really possible, or was she now being a fantasist too?

"Please someone, anyone, just explain these dreams

to me; am I having premonitions, or is it all fantasy?"

Speaking the words out loud, but with nobody to hear them, Kellie felt somewhat silly. But she was also desperate and wished whole-heartedly for it to be the latter, already feeling worried about what might happen in her next dream.

During the last two weeks, the dreams had slowly escalated day by day. It was as if Kellie was being drip-fed information, which she was supposed to pull together to make some kind of sense out of. But right now, none of it made any sense, or even seemed to be linked. Feeling decidedly emotional and actually quite scared, this was different to how Kellie was used to feeling upon wakening. She was definitely a bit out of sorts and almost felt like she was being urged to do something really important.

Remembering back to what her grandmother had told her many years ago – which at the time she had never really understood – Kellie was beginning to question if that was actually now coming true? Back then, despite not understanding fully, the young Kellie had taken on-board the notion that had been put to her, which was that she would develop some kind of psychic ability and do good things when she was older. Although Kellie often wondered what form that supposed ability would take, she also wondered how on earth her grandmother could have known, or foreseen, whatever it was that had convinced the older woman of Kellie's future. Unfortunately, with her grandmother having passed several years ago, the answer to that question remained a mystery to Kellie.

Feeling determined and forcing herself to stop thinking about the dreams, Kellie sat up and purposely threw back the thin bed-covers, to step out onto the soft pile rug covering the boarded floor beside her bed. Padding across the room to pull aside the obscure window drapery and slipping the catch undone, she gently pushed open the French doors. As her little home was basked in the morning sunlight, Kellie's mood lifted and smiling at the beauty of the day, she stepped out onto the veranda of her tiny beach-side house. It was already a gorgeous day and breathing in the warm sea air, Kellie turned her face towards the sun, which was shining brightly across the sparkling bay. As the sun's rays touched her face, she smiled again. Pure happiness, pleasure and contentment filled Kellie's soul. She delighted in how much she loved her little home, always feeling very appreciative of how fortunate she was to own it. The freshly painted wooden veranda was Kellie's most favourite place to sit in the mornings.

After taking a few moments to enjoy just being right there and feeling free from all worries and concerns, Kellie stepped back inside to make her morning coffee before returning to relax on one of the wooden chairs that welcomed visitors to her veranda.

As she sat sipping her coffee and looking out over the calm waters, Kellie watched the tiny surges on the surface as they formed into baby waves that rippled towards the water's edge and gently lapped the sandy shoreline. The scene created a sense of peaceful calmness within Kellie and it was a view she was extremely grateful for. It truly was her perfect location.

Kellie lifted her hand to acknowledge some local fishermen as they pushed their small boat out for the mid-morning catch, whilst hoping that a shoal of fish had been brought in closer to land by the returning tide. It was a daily activity that Kellie had watched and enjoyed so many times, yet it always gave her a sense of comfortable belonging and hopefulness of a good catch to fill the fishermen's nets. Weekends had never been better and Kellie loved her relaxed life, living here in her little beach-house, on the edge of Rosada Beachtown.

Unlike some of the larger houses which were randomly scattered along the shoreline, Kellie's wooden house was a very small, single storey building and with the exception of the bathroom, was pretty much open-plan in its design. A large double bed occupied one side of the main room and the row of cupboards running along the middle conveniently screened her bedroom area. The small kitchenette was tucked into one corner, along with a table and chairs, perfect for two, but capable of seating four. A small sofa-bed fitted in perfectly with Kellie's old and much-loved, big comfy armchair. Nothing particularly matched, but that didn't faze Kellie because she loved the eclectic feel of her cosy little home. Since living there, Kellie had added a small display unit, which now contained a slightly meagre collection of books and Jack's old vinyl collection (something she just could not bring herself to throw away). There was also a very small TV, which sat comfortably next to an old record deck, that had also belonged to her benefactor. Kellie often enjoyed playing Jack's record collection which, more often than not, was whenever Tom came over. It was Jack who had originally owned the small wooden house, with its blue wash-painted walls.

Having lived the vast majority of his life there, Jack had earned a simple living as one of the local fisherman. Many of the residents of Rosada Beachtown knew Jack and he thrived on being that well-known, and much-loved, local character. He was someone who often befriended the holiday-makers that returned each year, to visit their sleepy beachside town, which was also how he had first met Kellie's family. It was here too, in this beautiful place, that Jack had taught the young Kellie to fish and enjoy the many benefits of childhood summer-holidays. Kellie and her childhood friend Tom had often accompanied old Jack whenever he went out fishing for the afternoon catch, coming back thrilled whenever they too had caught a fish.

Ever since Kellie had been a toddler, her parents had rented the same summer holiday house, one that stood just along the beach from Jack's own little place.   So,   it was inevitable that over the years, the family grew to know and love old Jack as if he were one of their own kin. Equally, Jack had loved their little family and very much looked forward to their visits each summer.

Having lost his own wife and daughter during childbirth, many years previously, Jack had always looked upon Kellie as if she were his own little girl, proudly watching her grow from a child into the lovely young woman that she became. So, it was not surprising that Kellie had been left reeling with shock and disbelief when Jack suddenly passed away. She had cried for days, knowing, but not wanting to believe, that her beloved friend was gone forever and she mourned Jack's loss more than anyone else.

The shock of Jack's death was followed by more unexpected news. It was a couple of months later that Kellie's family were astounded to hear from a lawyer, who invited them to his office and advised them that Jack – who had no living relatives – had bequeathed his beach-side home to Kellie. Utterly amazed, Kellie and her parents had listened carefully as the lawyer relayed Jack's wishes, which were documented in his will. Their thoughts, still full of sadness at losing their dear friend, had merged with disbelief on hearing such unexpected news. By the time the lawyer had finished speaking and the news had sunk in, Kellie had felt completely overwhelmed by the fact that Jack had thought so highly of her. Tears had filled her eyes and her heart ached with the pain of losing Jack.

In the following days, excitement took over, as the news sunk in. It was true, the beach house and all of its contents now belonged to Kellie! Ever since that day, Kellie had regularly sent up happy thoughts to her dear friend Jack, hoping that wherever he was, he would somehow know how eternally grateful she was. Also hoping that he would like what she had done with the place since becoming its new owner, having made small improvements to put her own stamp on it.

In honour of her much-loved friend and as a thank you to him, Kellie had re-named the little house to *Jack's Place.* Additionally, she had decided that rather than continue with the busy city life, which was her familiar daily routine, she had wanted to escape and lead the happy, relaxed way of life that her little beach-house offered and which Jack himself had enjoyed for so many years. Kellie was moving to Rosada Beachtown!

During the following weeks, Kellie became the proud new resident owner of the little blue house. Not that she'd had very much to move into her new home. In fact, mostly it had been just a few personal belongings, a couple of new rugs and some bits and pieces of kitchen-ware, which she had mixed in with Jack's own random collection of china, pots and pans. Being so small, the house didn't really need much else and in Kellie's opinion, all it required was some love and a good dose of appreciation from its new owner.

As a house-warming gift, Kellie's parents, Barbara and Paul, had bought several tins of paint and together, the three of them re-decorated the whole place, just exactly the way Kellie wanted it. They even refreshed the outside, re-painting all of the external woodwork and veranda railings. In fact, the three of them had spent two weeks sprucing the place up. Cleaning and scrubbing every nook and cranny and generally giving the little house a brand-new lease of life inside and out.

Jack's Place was a perfect haven of peace and tranquillity and Kellie loved every last wooden slat that made-up her small and comfortable home; thanks to Jack, the future looked bright and aside from the still painful loss of her dearest friend, Kellie was happier than she ever imagined she could be.

On the final day of painting, the three of them sat and enjoyed a meal on the veranda, basking in the last of the evening sunshine, before it retreated below the horizon. They celebrated Kellie's new home with champagne. Clinking their glasses as they filled them with bubbles, the little family toasted their dear friend Jack to thank him again for his incredible gift to Kellie and for the years of friendship they had all shared. Then it was Kellie's turn to be toasted, as her parents wished her much love, laughter and happiness in her new home!

Being already familiar with the town that sprawled inland behind her little house had been a massive bonus and Kellie had felt right at home from the moment she took up residence. Both of her parents had agreed that it seemed as if this was all meant to be, when a few days later she was offered and took up a job in the town. Luckily for Kellie, her timing to move couldn't have been more perfect. It was a job she had felt excited about from the first moment of knowing she would be working there, because she would be working alongside her childhood friend Tom; the two of them upcycling furniture no longer wanted by the original owners. It was a store that Kellie knew well and had always been fascinated by throughout her childhood – it was like an emporium – mixing antiques with newer pieces, each celebrating a difference in style and having its own story to tell. The unusual store also held a selection of different shaped mirrors, odd table lamps and a small collection of battered leather-covered books and suitcases. Kellie had always liked to look through the books and myriad of trinkets, some of which were ornamental, whilst others were regimental medals. Kellie's fascination was always captured by wondering about the personal histories belonging to each piece; many of which were found in long-forgotten trunks, lying abandoned and unknown in people's attics and cellars, often covered in dust, before finding their way to the little store that Kellie had now joined.

Tom, like Kellie with *Jack's Place*, now owned the store, having also been fortunate enough to inherit it. On this occasion, however, the benefactor had been his own Great-Aunt Lilly, who, very much like Jack, had also been something of a local character in her day. Lilly had always encouraged Tom to spend as much time as he wanted to in her store and ever since he was a small boy, she had loved to show him how everything was made and worked, teaching him as she herself mended and made many pieces of furniture. Of course, being around the town every summer, meant that Kellie and Tom had grown up together and the two friends had regularly pestered Lilly, wanting to know about every new item that came in through the traditional glass panelled door.

During those childhood summer holidays, whenever they had not been with Lilly, the two young friends could be found swimming in the calm waters of the bay, or sitting on the beach near Jack's boat, waiting for him to take them both out fishing. Life had been simple for the two youngsters back then and it was that simplicity which they each longed for again.

Great-Aunt Lilly had sadly passed away five years previously, after a short and unexpected illness and although normally a strong character, it had devastated Tom to lose her. Despite feeling eternally grateful that Lilly hadn't suffered for too long and because Tom loved his aunt dearly, he had struggled to cope with losing the only family he had known as an adult and grieved her loss for a very long time. His only comfort came from knowing that Lilly would have hated to be a burden on Tom with a long drawn out illness, so whilst her passing was sudden and very quick, even he had to admit, that to go so fast had been the best possible way for his wonderful aunt.

Old Jack had also felt the pain of losing his dear friend Lilly, who had been such a tower of strength and support for him, throughout the years since losing his own beautiful bride. That terrible loss had occurred during what should have been one of the happiest moments of Jack's life; his darling Miranda had been lost whilst giving birth to their baby daughter, Hannah. Jack's beloved wife had suffered major complications during the premature birth of their baby girl – due to the emergency situation they had found themselves in, rather than being in the safety of the hospital, which was some forty odd miles away, they had been at home. A local doctor who rushed to attend to them had been unable to save either Miranda, or their baby daughter. It had been such a very sad time, which had touched their small community deeply, many having known the happy couple well.

In the years following the tragic loss of Miranda and Hannah, a glimmer of happiness had returned, as Lilly and Jack became and remained the dearest of friends. The two of them each missed Miranda terribly, yet in truth, they had been a great comfort to each other throughout that most painful time in their lives. As the years passed, many of the townsfolk hoped the two of them would eventually marry, but they never did. They just stayed the very dearest of friends, looking out for and helping each other whenever it was needed.

It had taken Tom almost four years to bounce back from losing Lilly, but since then, with Kellie's help, he'd turned their little store around and the business now had a regular flow of customers. Thanks to Lilly's years of teaching, Tom had become quite skilled when it came to carpentry and wood carving. A line of trade which benefitted their store greatly, was a long-time family trait that Lilly had been very proud of and equally keen to pass on to Tom, the next generation of their family duo.

Despite it having been unusual for a woman to

perform carpentry work, in what was traditionally a man's world back then, Lilly had absolutely loved the creativity of it all and had been well known locally as one of the best in the trade.

Picking up where Lilly left off, had Tom also repairing furniture and more recently, creating hand-carved statuettes of animals. Living in a town of dog-lovers, it wasn't long before Tom had received several commission requests from various local people. Between carving these statuettes and re-vamping the store, he had been kept very busy, which was something that had helped him enormously in his recovery after losing Lilly.

Kellie was always excited whenever new items came into the store and she lovingly handled each piece, cleaning and restoring them to their former glory as best she could, whilst wondering about the stories each could tell. Being a bit of a romantic and with quite a vivid imagination, Kellie always leaned towards imagining that their histories were happy ones and often – for her own amusement and when she didn't actually already know the original history – Kellie would attach her own interesting story to the more unusual pieces, as she imagined who the original owner was and what they had been like when the piece had belonged to them. It was a form of daydreaming that Tom often got caught up in, as the two of them made-up many unlikely stories, often laughing at each other's wild thoughts and ideas.

Tom absolutely loved what he did and grew to also enjoy the delighted reaction he received from his many happy and satisfied customers, as he unveiled yet another wood carving of a much-loved pet. On the underside of each carving Tom always carefully chiselled his initials; a simple TC, for Tom Chandler. Kellie was amazed at Tom's wood-working skills and she often told him he was just like Lilly, which made him visibly glow and grin with unashamed pride. Tom loved to be compared to his aunt and he hoped that Lilly, wherever she was, would be very proud of what he had achieved so far. One thing Tom knew for sure was, how much Lilly would have approved of the fact that he and Kellie were now working together, successfully continuing with their family business so well.

Tom and Kellie were like a brother and sister who always had each other's backs and often found that even their thoughts were in tune, realising they knew what the other was thinking, or about to say. The two friends shared so much with each other, including their hopes and dreams for the future, as well as those for their little store. So, unsurprisingly, it was in Tom that Kellie usually confided and in particular, about her recent strange dreams. Never one to mock, Tom always took Kellie's concerns about her dreams seriously, but he also worried that the dreams themselves might take over her already vivid imagination.

Feeling like a responsible protector, Tom always listened intently, often keeping Kellie grounded with his fairly solid advice, whilst supporting her over the strange dreams. After all, he was very aware that *she* had been the one to save *him* from the depths of depression after Lilly had died, which had been a long haul. Kellie had never once faltered in her support of Tom, and whilst he was much better now and could look back on his time with his great-aunt as more precious than any material thing could ever be, Tom acknowledged his recovery was accelerated thanks to Kellie's constant encouragement. It seemed like the two of them were perfect partners in life, as well as when it came to running the store.

Their love of recycling the old and blending it with the new style of living that people adopted nowadays, meant they were a popular partnership in their little community. Attracting customers who would enjoy browsing and lingering for slightly longer than they'd intended, as they passed the time of day with Tom and Kellie, before then buying whatever something had caught their eye.

Whenever an owner brought an item into their little store to sell, Tom and Kellie would always listen patiently and intently to every shared story about the history of whatever was being offered. This small gesture made the owners of those items feel that their possessions were being utterly appreciated and cared for, even before being sold to an equally worthy recipient. It was this special talent and subconscious natural empathy that Tom and Kellie seemed to have, which drew people to them constantly, enabling their unusual little store to thrive.

Chapter 2

Life with Tom

Monday started well, the sunrise was spectacular and the early morning fishermen were already out in the bay. Sitting outside with her morning coffee, Kellie watched as the small fishing boat, now far out in the bay, bobbed along on the sparkling water. With her feet on the opposite chair, Kellie was feeling totally relaxed and contented, before returning inside to get showered and dressed for a new day in the little store that she loved so much. As she got ready for work, Kellie hummed a bygone tune which popped into her head subconsciously.

Meanwhile, above that same store, Tom had not long woken up. Unusually for him, he had overslept ever so slightly and was now rushing to shave and shower before work. Without knowing it, the two of them were mirroring each other's actions, even down to humming the same tune, before eating a quick slice of toast and honey to kick-start their working day.

Kellie had taken to cycling to the store, which meant she could enjoy taking in the scenic route, as she casually peddled past the other beach houses before turning up Long Street, which was the main shopping street stretching up through the town and a couple more blocks past their own little store. The town had grown from a small beach-side community with barely a smattering of stores and houses, into a settlement of several thousand people and was still growing. This was mainly due to the many visitors who came and often settled in the town, as well as the natural expansion of its own population – children grew and had families themselves. Luckily for Tom and Kellie, the town was just about big enough to sustain their store, which was growing ever popular for

Tom's hand-carved animal statuettes, as much as the eclectic collection of pre-loved belongings and newer items they sold.

While Kellie cycled up the hill, Tom turned the sign on the door to show they were open for business. Although they rarely had customers in before ten o'clock – like his Aunt Lilly – Tom always liked to show consistency by keeping to the advertised times clearly displayed on the glass window of the main door. Those times aside, both Tom and Kellie would often start early and work later – well past closing time – as the two of them were often totally engrossed in their restoration work. With very few outside commitments for either of them, the flexible hours suited both Kellie and Tom perfectly and the two friends loved working together. They often spent their free time at the store, where work never seemed like work, because they had so much fun together. The two of them loved exploring and improving everything that came to them, both through the donated items, as well as those they purchased directly from the original owners.

It was looking like they were in for a busy Monday. Tom had a chair to fix and then had to finish off two statuette orders he'd been working on over the weekend, so he was happy to leave Kellie to mind the store whilst he continued fixing, sanding and oiling the wood. The work-room in the back of the store was Tom's most favourite place to be and his love of working with wood – the smell and feel of it – always brought him joy; he loved making new things, as well as renovating old pieces. Which suited Kellie perfectly, because she liked to do the cleaning, oiling and polishing side of things; her work being equally important in attracting the right buyer. It was a convenience which made them the ideal working duo.

In fact, it was only recently and much to her surprise, that Kellie found she was quite good at fixing the more delicate and fiddly pieces that came in. Although, she still often wondered quite how she knew what to do to fix some things. Kellie was very aware that her only experience had come from watching Tom and of course, Lilly, during their childhood summers. It was obvious that Kellie was developing new skills. The two of them liked to think it was because Lilly was watching over them and somehow guiding them both, gently nudging their minds and hands to find the best ways to fix things. It brought the young friends great comfort to think of Lilly still being around them and helping in this way.

The latest item to have been donated to their store was an old wardrobe trunk from the mid to late 1800s and which, to their great delight, had a small brown leather suitcase tucked away inside it, hidden in the bottom of the drawer side of the trunk. Both the trunk and suitcase were clearly in need of some love and attention, which would fall into Kellie's working domain. Since arriving, they had been left sitting in a corner of the work-room, waiting for her to find time to start restoring them as closely as possible to their former glory – and today was going to be that very day. Despite not being able to open the smaller case due to a seized lock, it was the antique wardrobe trunk which most appealed to Kellie. The hide exterior had long since seen better days, but with Lilly's magic mixture (a recipe she had left for Tom), the hide was reviving so well that once Kellie had cleaned it up and polished the metal corners and hinges, she knew the trunk would look really impressive once the restoration was finished. Realistically, neither Tom nor Kellie thought anyone would actually buy the heavy old trunk to use for travelling nowadays. After all, it was more suited to the old times, when steamers were a common method of travel. But it was fair to say, they both loved the antique trunk and hoped that maybe someone with a similar love of old things, might just like to own it and use it in a guest room, or even display it as a novelty talking piece.

There certainly were plenty of suitable houses around Rosada Beachtown which were old enough to contain many items of a similar age to their trunk, so they supposed there could possibly be someone out there who would love it. Although Tom said that even if they didn't manage to sell it, he'd keep it in the store anyway, just for the novelty factor. Kellie agreed and felt sure that as not many people would have seen such an interesting trunk from the days of steamer travel, it might generate much interest and intrigue as to its history.

Kellie was still polishing away at the trunk's hide when the store's old-fashioned door-bell tinkled, indicating that a customer had arrived. Putting down her messy cloth and removing the protective gloves she wore, Kellie walked through to find their dear old friend, Mrs Terry, browsing the glass cabinet containing a random collection of antique looking jewellery. Mrs Terry had been one of Great-Aunt Lilly's oldest and closest friends, who often popped into the store to check on Lilly's nephew and his lovely friend, both of whom she was so fond of. Secretly though the other reason for her frequent visits was to feel close to the energy of her dear old friend who was no longer there, but who had once stood behind that very display cabinet, now doubling as a counter.

Kellie brightened at the sight of her favourite customer: "Good morning, Mrs Terry. How are you today?"

"Ah, my dear, good morning to you too. I'm very well thank you, Kellie. Mustn't complain must we."

The older lady smiled broadly, causing Kellie to beam back at her as she replied again, "Are you looking for something particular, or would you just like to browse today?"

"Well actually, my dear, I was looking for a brooch,

two of mine have broken clasps and I need one for my new jacket. I've been invited to a family wedding you know; my youngest niece is getting married, so I'm travelling over to the Benzene quarter to join in the celebrations." Charlotte Terry was positively beaming with pride at this piece of news.

Kellie smiled and said how lovely it would be to go to a wedding, just as Mrs Terry continued with more exciting news, "Did you know our family have recently struck oil, Kellie? It turns out there's quite a lot of it down there, so everyone is very excited of course. Mind you, not that I need to be worrying about all that. I'm quite happy with my life as it is and I don't want to change it, but it will be so lovely for my sister's family to have the financial security it will bring. I guess that will last them for the rest of their lives. If the oil doesn't run out of course." Mrs Terry chuckled. "It will be so wonderful for my niece and her new husband too, don't you think? They'll start their married life together with no financial worries about the future."

The 'don't you think' was more of a statement than a question really, but Kellie was very comfortable chatting with Mrs Terry and so she responded enthusiastically.

"Oh, that sounds absolutely fabulous for them, Mrs Terry, and no, I didn't know. How exciting, they must be completely thrilled to be starting their married life with such a lucky beginning!"

Seeing a proud stance in Mrs Terry, Kellie realised her favourite customer was genuinely excited for her younger relatives. Equally, Kellie also absolutely understood Charlotte Terry in not wanting to change her own life by moving upstate and joining her soon-to-be-wealthy relatives. The life they all shared in Rosada Beachtown was so lovely that nobody wanted to change it by moving away. Mrs Terry chatted on as she glanced into the glass display cabinet: "I'm sure they are bouncing off the walls with excitement, Kellie my dear. They worked long and hard and have been drilling for a long time. Thankfully, it seems their determination has finally paid off for them." Pausing, Charlotte Terry pointed into the cabinet. "Now then, I quite like this brooch here, the green one. Don't you think with the light shining on the stones, they look just like emeralds and small diamonds?"

Kellie had to agree that whilst the stones did look remarkably similar to the precious gems they were emulating, all of them were in fact imitation and therefore not worth anywhere near as much as the real thing would be. But, she had to agree, the brooch was totally in-keeping with the type of jewellery that Mrs Terry liked to wear. It would look perfect pinned onto the lapel of her new jacket.

Charlotte Terry looked back at Kellie and smiled again: "Yes, it's very pretty and reflects the light well. I think I'll take it please, Kellie, and if you have a little bag for it that would be lovely, my dear."

"Certainly, Mrs Terry. In fact I have a gorgeous little presentation box in our workshop, which will set it off perfectly, I'll just pop and fetch it for you."

As she came back with a pretty green box, Kellie invited Mrs Terry to bring her broken brooches in, so that she could take a look at them and see if they could easily be repaired by herself or Tom, or if they would indeed need to go to a professional jeweller.

"Thank you, Kellie, you're very kind to me, my dear. You know our Lilly would have been so proud to see you and Tom working here together. I miss her every day as you know, but, just popping in here cheers me right up again." Looking intently at Kellie, she added: "I know she's around and watching over us all, I'm sure she's making sure we don't get into any mischief." With that, the older lady winked and chuckled; her voice still had a youthful tone and it reminded Kellie of the times she'd seen Lilly and Charlotte Terry together, the two of them often laughing at some shared little secret. Smiling as she held open the door for Mrs Terry, Kellie was pleased with the sale and knew the brooch would make their dear friend feel so special for the big day. Plus of course, it had made their store a nice little profit.

Returning to the back-room where Tom was working, Kellie relayed the news about Mrs Terry's family striking oil and along with the surprise at such news, Tom agreed how amazing it was for them and how lucky it was for the newly-weds to start their married life together during such exciting family times. Although, like Mrs Terry, the two friends also agreed that they wouldn't want to swap their own peaceful and happy lives for the glitz and glamour that oil riches would inevitably bring.

As the day wore on, the two friends were kept busy, both working on individual items and serving customers in-between until finally, Kellie stated that she was done. It had to be said that the trunk looked amazing again, with its re-nourished hide and shiny polished corners. Tom was impressed. Remarkably the interior had needed very little attention, other than a quick clean. The old trunk had obviously been well cared for in its day and having languished unused and covered up in a loft, for so many years, the interior was virtually immaculate. It was very old of course, but in the main, undamaged, with its hanging rail on one side and set of drawers on the other. Following Kellie's hard work, it now looked remarkably well preserved. This was a piece that both Kellie and Tom decided absolutely *must* have a romantic history and so they began imagining its story. As Kellie picked up the small brown leather suitcase that had been hidden inside the bottom drawer of the heavy wardrobe trunk, she shook it gently.

"You know, Tom, for a small case, this feels quite heavy... there must be something inside it."

After a bit of oiling and tweaking, much to both hers and Tom's delight, Kellie somehow managed to release the seized catch on the small suitcase. They both watched with excited anticipation at what might be inside. Kellie gently lifted the lid and laid it backwards, so they could both see the disguised contents of the little suitcase. Whatever it was, it seemed to be very well packaged, with several layers of yellowed tissue paper covering the contents. Pulling the loose paper back, away from what it was covering, the two of them could see an odd shaped object, also obscured by yellowed tissue paper wrapped carefully around it and packed in with more of the same scrunched up paper. Someone had gone to great lengths to protect whatever it was that the package held. Looking at how well preserved it was, encouraged anticipated thoughts of something of value by both Tom and Kellie. As she gently picked out the object and began unwrapping its protective covering, the two friends felt their anticipation growing.

Kellie spoke first: "Isn't this exciting, Tom. I wonder what it is." Kellie pulled the final paper covering away and couldn't hide her delight as she held up the item, both of them in awe, as their eyes inspected it carefully.

"Oh my goodness, it looks really old. Wow, are those Egyptian symbols? Kellie, do you suppose this trunk has travelled to Egypt on the old steamers that sailed along the Suez Canal back in the day? Oh, how exciting is this. I mean, WOW!" Tom was gabbling as Kellie stood staring at it, almost speechless. Having studied ancient Egyptian history at university, Kellie was almost beside herself to think that they quite possibly held a piece of ancient Egyptian treasure in their hands.

It was a golden coloured goblet, obviously hand crafted, but very fine for its time and quite ornate. There were four black stones set around the sides, with Egyptian hieroglyphics etched around the rim and on the base of the stem. The golden goblet was truly amazing. Both Kellie and Tom were awestruck by its beauty and neither of them said anything as they first looked at each other, then back to the goblet.

"We have to find the owner of this suitcase, Kellie. We have to return this. They couldn't possibly have known what was inside it and have obviously given this to us by mistake." Tom voiced what Kellie had thought, but she felt strangely attracted to the goblet and didn't want to put it down. Instead, she passed it to Tom, who gently took it into his own hands. He too felt an instant attraction, something strange and not what he had expected to feel, which also fazed him slightly. The two friends could not remove their gaze from this amazing treasure, which had so mysteriously ended up in their possession. Yet both of them recognised and accepted that they could not possibly keep the golden goblet. Tom and Kellie both knew instinctively, they absolutely had to find the owner of the suitcase, and quickly.

Thanks to Kellie's organised record keeping, it was a task which would not prove too difficult for them. Since Kellie had first begun working with Tom, she had kept a clear record of who donated each item, which ones they had paid for, along with who eventually bought the item and the amount it was sold for. Kellie also kept a note of any known history or information relating to each piece. All of her records were up to date and so it wasn't long before they identified the name and address of the person who had brought the old wardrobe trunk in. Kellie could remember that it had been a lady, because she had engaged the help of a couple of young lads, who had carried the heavy trunk in for her. She also recalled how the trunk had intrigued both her and Tom when it first landed on their floor. Discussing that moment again now, the two of them decided that because the trunk was already so heavy, neither the owner, or the two lads, probably even noticed the additional weight of the small brown suitcase that was hidden away in the bottom drawer.

The lady in question had been a Mrs Marjorie Brown, from Lincoln, who had only travelled to Rosada Beachtown to supervise the emptying of a property belonging to a distant and now deceased relative. Apparently, Marjorie Brown had not even known the existence of her benefactor, but their lawyers had traced a family link to her, which had been confirmed. The lawyers acting on behalf of the estate had advised Marjorie that as she seemed to be the only living relative of the deceased. The entire estate had been signed over to her. However, already a wealthy woman in her own right, whilst Marjorie had welcomed owning the house, she had wanted little to do with the multitude of random artefacts within it, which had been collected over a lifetime of her relative's travelling and were of no interest to her personally.

It seemed Marjorie's relative had been married to an archaeologist and the two of them had spent many years travelling around the Middle East gathering various pieces of paraphernalia. At least that is what it seemed like to Marjorie and she certainly had no interest in any of the artefacts. Having decided that none of it was worth very much in terms of real cash, Marjorie had turned benefactor herself and donated the whole collection to a museum, which she had located upstate and which specialised in Egyptian artefacts.

When Kellie and Tom called Marjorie Brown, her answering machine clicked on, meaning they had to leave a message asking Marjorie to please call them back regarding the old trunk that she'd left at their store. Both Tom and Kellie's hearts sank a little, as they realised they would probably only have the goblet in their possession for a short time. It was a fact which seemed to really

24

unsettle them and yet neither of them could explain why. The goblet held a strong attraction for them both and they really wanted to keep it, but as always, honesty was their policy and an ethic which had been ingrained into their DNA from a young age. So, there was no question of *not* returning the goblet to the rightful owner.

Two days passed and still there was no return call from Marjorie. When they tried her telephone number again, the call dropped to an answering service once more. This time Tom spoke and left the same message that Kellie had left two days earlier. He also repeated the telephone number for their store, before again asking Marjorie to please call them back.

Still no return call came and as the days went by, Tom and Kellie continued about their usual business. Customers came and went, whilst the goblet sat in pride of place in their workshop, just within reach, so they could pick it up and touch it whenever they felt the urge to do so. As each day passed, they both felt relieved that Marjorie Brown hadn't yet called back, whilst at the same time, dreading the moment when she would. So much so, that every time the telephone rang, they would glance quickly at each other, both wondering the same thing, was this it – *the call.* Was it Marjorie?

In fact, it was a full eight days before Marjorie finally returned their call, apologising profusely for the delay in responding and explaining that she had been out of town on business. Tom answered the telephone and waved madly at Kellie, pointing to the receiver, mouthing *it's her* to Kellie's now disappointed face. Tom explained to Marjorie about the small suitcase and finding the goblet, describing what it looked like and what they thought it could be, before then asking Marjorie if she would like them to send it on to her, or if she would prefer to collect it.

Marjorie remembered the fiasco she'd experienced

when clearing all of the other artefacts from her relative's house and groaned internally. Knowing that she didn't want the goblet herself, Marjorie also realised that she would have to arrange for someone to take it upstate to pass it on to the Egyptian museum. So, no, Marjorie told a shocked Tom, it wasn't worth her worrying about collecting a single goblet and that seeing as Tom seemed to like it so much, he should keep it himself.

At least that's the story Marjorie told Tom. The real worry for her was that the museum had said some of the artefacts looked like they may have come from an Egyptian tomb. The Museum Curator had then gone on to explain how, in the early part of the twentieth century, such items often had rumour of a curse attached to them. A claim to which Marjorie had recoiled from and being an extremely superstitious woman herself, she had been relieved to offload everything to the museum. Particularly so after having been advised by the lawyers, that the husband of her recently deceased relative had himself died a painful and untimely death, apparently after returning from Egypt back in the early 1900s. On finding that out, Marjorie had really wanted nothing more to do with the artefacts, so yes, she was more than happy to leave the goblet with Tom and Kellie.

When Tom came off the phone, he could scarcely believe their luck and with a look of disbelief, he just nodded to Kellie, signalling that yes, they could keep the goblet. Squealing with excitement, Kellie and Tom hugged each other and danced around the work-room table, such was their utter relief and delight at being the new owners of the ancient goblet. For they were sure it was ancient and probably worth a small fortune. Not that either of them had any inclination to sell it. No, they were keeping it and where it sat right now, was going to be the golden goblet's new home.

As they packed-up the store for the night, Tom

decided he would lock the goblet away in the safe and then take it out each morning, which Kellie agreed was probably a good idea. Not that there was much danger of the store being broken into; the crime rate in Rosada Beachtown was virtually non-existent. However, they did have visitors to the town who were people they didn't know and decided it was best to be cautious, each of them subconsciously thinking that now the goblet was theirs, there was no way they wanted to risk losing it.

The evening was a balmy one and so the two young friends decided to pick up something to eat and go back to Kellie's place. They were in such a joyful mood that instead of pushing Kellie's bike home with them, Tom sat astride it and suggested she sit on the cross-bar. It was just as if they were children again and playing in their summer holidays. The two of them wobbled and giggled all the way back to the beach-house that was now Kellie's home. Sitting out on the veranda eating their food and drinking several glasses of wine, they reflected on the week's events and their luck at keeping the goblet. It had been an amazing day and their excitement could hardly be contained, evident by their equally frantic chatter. As the night wore on and the effect of several glasses of wine kicked in, Tom asked Kellie if her dreams had settled down, or if any of the details had joined up and made any sense to her yet?

The answer to that was a firm NO as Kellie confirmed that they definitely had NOT settled down and in fact the unusual dreams were becoming ever more frequent, but the information was so random that it made no sense at all to Kellie. However, she was relieved to admit the good news was, that she no longer felt unsettled or anxious about them. That at least, was a positive sign and one that Tom was happy to hear. He had secretly become increasingly worried about Kellie's dreams over the past few weeks.

As they finished their evening of food, wine and excited chatter, Tom stated that he'd best say goodnight and get back home. Although the following day was Sunday, whilst the store would be closed, he wanted to work on one of his wood carvings, adding for Kellie to be sure to call if she needed him for anything at all.

Kellie smiled at Tom and thanked him for that, but, she reminded him, she had nothing more strenuous planned, than to tidy her front garden and lay out under the dappled shade of the tree to read her book. Although, Kellie admitted, that with the soft sound of the lapping water, it was quite likely she would end up dozing rather than reading in the warmth of the afternoon sunshine.

Kissing Tom goodbye on each cheek, she watched as he walked off down the pathway to the quiet beach road, which was about a hundred yards from where Kellie stood. Turning to wave a final goodbye to Kellie, Tom walked around the corner and wandered home in the balmy evening air. Yes, he was very happy and Kellie was happy, and that was all that mattered to Tom as he smiled up at the moon.

Chapter 3

Egypt

Stepping back inside *Jack's Place*, Kellie marvelled at her good fortune to be living right by the water's edge, in this gorgeous little beach house and to have Tom in her life. *He is such a good friend*, she thought. Although it was not lost on Kellie that they had never become boyfriend and girlfriend, somehow, romance had never been the route for them. They had been happy to be friends ever since they were small children and that was how it had seemed their life would be, which was perfectly fine by her because Tom meant the world to Kellie and she wanted him to be in her life forever. Tom made her feel safe, loved and protected. She in turn, loved that about him.

As Kellie washed and dried the last of the dishes they'd used that evening, she looked out of the window and across the bay, towards the horizon. The moon was unusually bright this evening and it prompted Kellie to dry her hands and go back out onto the veranda, to gaze up at the night sky. Wow! It really was an amazing night. The sky was a deep midnight blue, which turned into an inky blackness as you moved your eye away from the brilliant whiteness of the moon, which displayed a circular aura in the sky surrounding it. A perfect moment to make a wish Kellie thought and as she stared up at the brilliant moon, she wished to know more about the golden goblet which had come into their possession so easily. Having stood for a good ten minutes, Kellie felt a cool breeze pass her as she turned to go back inside, but sub-consciously dismissed it. Having tidied everything away and crossing back to the windows, Kellie pulled the curtains closed and switched off the lamps in the living area, before making her way to her bed and undressing. Turning down the bed-covers, she slid between the soft, silky sheets and leant across to flick the switch on her bedside lamp. As the room plunged into semi-darkness, the light of the moon seemed bright against the obscure curtains. Kellie's eyes accustomed to the change in light as they were drawn towards the brightness. Lying in the soft moonlight, she thought about the golden goblet and how lucky she and Tom were to be its new owners. Closing her eyes, Kellie let out a small sigh as her mind calmed and willed her to sleep; drifting voluntarily, she was unable to resist the urge of unconscious rest which beckoned so strongly.

As the night wore on, sleeping peacefully by the ocean, Kellie's dreams became her reality and it was as if she had stepped back in time, now walking in the shoes of Jocelyn, a beautiful young Egyptian woman, who had lived a happy life, but who had now fallen in love with the wrong man. Jocelyn's unrequited love burned intensely for her bodyguard, a strong man who originated from a place outside of Egypt. Hailing from a forbidden land, this striking man had recently come to the attention of Jocelyn's mistress, Cleopatra. Ibrahim was big and very strong, with the earned might of a Roman Gladiator. Known as *Ibrahim the Black* and just as his name suggested, he was dark-skinned, a warrior champion and the newly chosen protector for Jocelyn. None other than Cleopatra herself had chosen Ibrahim to protect her most precious and favoured subject.

With the exception of her latest lover, Samson, whom Cleopatra adored, her only other regular companion was Jocelyn, who was most precious to her mistress. Regarding her subject as second only in beauty to Cleopatra herself, the Lady Jocelyn was divine, her skin was as pure as porcelain and her eyes captivating, the colour of which could only be described as an inky blue and unlike any others. Just like Ibrahim, Cleopatra adored

Jocelyn. The two women were inseparable and spent many hours and days together, talking and grooming, as they also discussed matters of state. It was Cleopatra's willingness to take counsel and suggestions from Jocelyn, which stirred up angst and dismay among the members of Cleopatra's closest court and old guard. This friendship and sharing of court matters was frowned upon by many, but none of whom would dare to raise their concerns to Cleopatra, for fear of reprisal.

Yet these two women were very astute, both Cleopatra and Jocelyn each very well aware of the jealousies of the other court members and old guards. Those jealousies being the main reason that Cleopatra felt the need for Jocelyn to be protected by *Ibrahim the Black*. In the weeks that passed, neither woman had known or expected that love would grow between protector and his protected, but being thrown together meant that love's seed truly was sown and the two of them were soon to become lovers. They hid their feelings well, or so they had thought, but true love is easily detected by those who are keen to watch carefully. Looking for signs and just a few weeks into Ibrahim's arrival, the old guards noted exchanged looks between the Lady Jocelyn and Ibrahim the Warrior Champion. The time they spent alone together was limited, controlled by the demands on Jocelyn's time by her mistress Cleopatra. It was only once the handsome and charming Samson had walked into court and indulged himself in Cleopatra's intimate life, that Jocelyn began to find herself with more free time.

During that free time Ibrahim watched his mistress closely as she smiled and talked and laughed. Jocelyn's smile could light up any place that she walked into and Ibrahim was extremely honoured and proud to be her protector. However, it was that same smile which was to be his downfall, as he fell hopelessly in love with his Egyptian goddess, his very own Lady Jocelyn. Ibrahim wanted her to be his. It was a forbidden love, because of his race, his background and current position; however, it was a love of the sweetest kind and Ibrahim was so good to Jocelyn, that she soon found herself willingly returning his loving attentions. On many a sunny and calm day, as they walked among the pillars of a small deserted ruin, which stood in the vast grounds of Cleopatra's home beside the River Nile, Jocelyn would ask Ibrahim about his life. When he recalled stories of the colosseum and the battles he'd fought, Jocelyn was impressed by his strength and his values. *Ibrahim the Black*, whilst a Warrior Champion, was also merciful and would not kill his opponents. Rather he would adopt the best ones into his legion of gladiators and train them to much higher standards. Kimea was one such opponent who had stood out from the rest and was the one that Ibrahim trained hardest, for he looked upon Kimea as a successor to him.

Jocelyn knew this man Ibrahim was her protector and therefore any kind of relationship would be forbidden, but she could not help herself and after several weeks of walking and sharing stories of their lives, Jocelyn's reserve wilted.

It was on one such occasion that Ibrahim was stood between the pillars of the same ruin they regularly walked around; his muscles were gleaming in the sunshine, having been massaged with oil that very morning. Without thinking, as the sunlight touched them, so Jocelyn too reached out and touched his arm with her fingertips. Ibrahim was strong and solid, but the touch of Jocelyn's hand melted his heart like it was made of butter. Her essence and her very being was overpowering to him, he could barely resist returning Jocelyn's touch, knowing that was not to be his decision. Struggling with his emotions and desires, he found strength from somewhere deep inside and held back. But the chemistry between them was strong and it sparkled as Jocelyn stood ever closer to Ibrahim. He could feel her breath on his skin as without warning, she took hold of his forearm to steady herself, then she, the Lady Jocelyn, stood on tiptoe and kissed Ibrahim's lips so tenderly. The Warrior Champion tried hard, but like any normal red-blooded male, he struggled to resist her wonderfully warm and soft lips. Finally, no longer able to hold himself back and unknowingly watched by Simona, both the protector and the protected, kissed each other deeply and passionately. Ibrahim's strong arms held Jocelyn close to him, his very soul burned with desire for this woman, with whom he had fallen so utterly and completely in love. In her arms he was weak, just an ordinary man, who could be taken by this woman's touch and kiss. It was more than he could bear and as Ibrahim swept Jocelyn up into his arms, he stepped inside the ruins.

Simona, who watched from behind the trees, knew what was about to happen and wept, for she too had fallen in love with Ibrahim, but had told no one. Simona's was a secret love, totally unrequited and it was more than she could bear as she ran away, crying out her pain with every step she took. Unbeknown to Jocelyn and Ibrahim, this woman would soon become a danger to the new lovers and their forbidden love.

Inside the ruins, Ibrahim stood Jocelyn on the soft greenness of the earth which filled this small oasis in the desert. Removing his cloak, he laid it on the ground for the two of them to lie upon. It was a warm and welcoming spot which had caught the last of the early evening sun. Taking Jocelyn's hand, Ibrahim admired her as she sank to the ground; she was so graceful and beautiful, yet her mind and lithe body were willing and wanting him to take her virginity. Ibrahim was a gentle lover and took his time to pleasure his Lady Jocelyn, until finally the two of them reached a passion so intense that it exploded inside of them both. And, just as the two became one, unknowingly, they had created a small life inside of Jocelyn's soft belly. Lying together, whilst the sun slowly dropped to the horizon, the two lovers held each other and talked of a life together as husband and wife. But it was a dream life which they also knew, would not be permitted by Cleopatra's Court. The two lovers knew that if they were to have any kind of future together, they would need to ask Cleopatra to grant them special permission, which they also knew would be difficult for their mistress. Because of their love for Cleopatra, they wanted to ease that burden for her and so instead, they plotted to run away together. The two lovers decided they would flee to Israel and share their lives together, living by the Sea of Galilee and far away from the courtiers and old guard that surrounded Cleopatra.

It was a dream they shared with much longing and one they would talk about at every opportunity, in every small moment alone that was granted to them. But Cleopatra's needs and demands were great and Jocelyn knew they had to bide their time before they could leave. For Jocelyn felt sure that Samson would soon become a long-term lover and companion for Cleopatra, meaning her services would no longer be required. As the months passed, so Jocelyn's belly grew and she realised that she was with child. Telling Ibrahim and seeing the pure joy on his face, made such news all the more beautiful for Jocelyn and as she blossomed, so did her deepening love for Ibrahim, along with his for her.

While the months passed, so the bitterness inside Simona grew and she plotted to end this union. Knowing the old guards wanted Ibrahim gone, she was tempted to tell them of what she had witnessed that day. But instead she waited and followed the two lovers as often as she dared, watching whenever and wherever they met, and shared their love, a love that she herself had wanted to receive from Ibrahim. Biding her time and nurturing her bitterness for her own unrequited feelings, on a particularly low day, Simona decided to tell one of the old guards of what she had witnessed. The most senior guard was Abraham and at her suggestion, he went with her one day. On seeing the two lovers together, Abraham was quietly surprised, but did nothing. Unbeknown to Simona, he was the only old guard who actually liked Ibrahim and respected him as a Warrior Champion. Unaware of her reasons for this betrayal, Abraham advised Simona to dismiss it and to let go of the concerns she held. This advice did not please Simona as she continued to plot her revenge. Abraham was her father and she had expected him to take up and join in with her intended disclosure. Simona was bitterly disappointed at her father's reaction and wise words, also knowing that she could not abide by his well-intentioned advice.

As the months passed, still Samson had not yet been accepted as Cleopatra's long-term companion. It was becoming more and more difficult for Jocelyn to hide her belly. The day finally came when she had to tell Cleopatra. It was a moment which terrified Jocelyn. As she expected, Cleopatra's first reaction was one of shock and disappointment, for Cleopatra knew that she would lose her most beloved companion. But thankfully, Jocelyn's fears of rejection by her mistress were unfounded, which was due to the fact that she too was in love. Cleopatra had understood Jocelyn's undeniable love for Ibrahim and so it was agreed that before their baby was born, Cleopatra would allow Jocelyn to leave her service to be with Ibrahim. Knowing how badly this decision would be taken by her own court, Cleopatra declared that she would delay her announcement until three months before the baby was due, at which time she would make it known that as their punishment, she, the great Cleopatra, was banishing the two lovers to another land. This would allow Ibrahim and Jocelyn time to escape to Israel and find a home by the Sea of Galilee, before their baby was born. Cleopatra wished for them both to live out their planned future together happily, as a family, and safe from the envy and hatred among her own courtiers. This dismissal of her most treasured companion would prove to her courtiers that Cleopatra also held compassion for those who served her well. It would clearly demonstrate that she could be merciful. This understanding was so greatly appreciated by both Jocelyn and Ibrahim, that the two of them remained as faithful as ever to their wise and gracious mistress.

But, before that time arrived, the old guard also noted the change in Jocelyn's body shape and they became even more restless and anxious, as their desperation grew to find out who the father of this unborn child was, so that they could discredit the two lovers to the court. In their jealous minds, they assumed that because the Lady Jocelyn had held a relationship in secret, they believed it must therefore mean it was a forbidden love. The old guard suspected the father was already betrothed. This false suspicion stirred their feelings of resentment towards Jocelyn even more.

Cleopatra had advised Jocelyn not to speak of her love for Ibrahim, to avoid the wrath of the old guard and any unnecessary danger to them both, whilst also warning them to be careful about whom they trusted. However, before the announcement could be made by Cleopatra and just seven months into the carrying term of her unborn child, Jocelyn was taken ill during the night. Unusually, Ibrahim was not close by, having been called away to check on one of Cleopatra's own guards, who had taken to his bed with a fever. It was to Ibrahim's utter regret that he wasn't with his beloved that night, when their baby daughter arrived into this world still-born. Jocelyn's cries could be heard across the palace. Those same cries brought Simona running to Jocelyn's chamber. On seeing the dark-skinned baby lying on the bed, still and lifeless, Simona was overcome with jealousy and rage. Crying out as she ran from Jocelyn's bed-chamber, a red-mist descended upon Simona's mind and she ran to find Ibrahim.

Ibrahim and the guard he was visiting had been drinking wine together when Abraham unexpectedly entered their chamber. With his fever now broken, the sick guard was feeling well enough to share the medicinal goblet of wine. As the two men looked at him, Abraham advised his Warrior Champion that a woman could be heard screaming and crying, and that whilst he could not be sure, the noise seemed to be coming from the Lady Jocelyn's quarters. As the shocked Ibrahim thanked the older man, he immediately jumped up to go and investigate, just as Simona also ran into the chamber. Startled and blinded with jealous fury, from beneath her robes, Simona withdrew a dagger and without delay, she plunged it into Ibrahim. Falling with him as the wound struck deep, Simona cried out, "It should have been me…"

Abraham lurched forward to pull his daughter away from the wounded Ibrahim, both men shocked that she would commit such an act. Abraham forced Simona away from Ibrahim and pulled her out of the chamber. As Ibrahim fell to the ground, the sick guard he had been tending to called for help. But none came. Several minutes later, a crying Jocelyn staggered into the chamber. Knowing where Cleopatra's guards usually rested, it had not been difficult for her to find the two men after hearing the sick guard's cries for help. Still losing blood from the birth, Jocelyn was holding their stillborn baby in her arms, the tiny body wrapped in a bloodied cloth. Seeing Ibrahim lying on the floor, his own blood joining with the spilt wine spreading out from his fallen golden goblet, Jocelyn screamed again, her despair was beyond anything she could have imagined. As she dropped to her knees, she placed their baby girl in Ibrahim's arms and poured water into the fallen goblet. Trying to help Ibrahim drink the water, Jocelyn wept. Seeing his blood flowing so fast, Jocelyn knew she was also about to lose the man she loved, as well as their new-born child. Ibrahim asked Jocelyn not to forget him, adding that he would always love her and protect her. With his dying breaths, he asked her to name their stillborn child Mary.

Gone were their dreams of being a family and living beside the Sea of Galilee. Gone was the man she loved and with him, the child they had made together.

As Jocelyn held Ibrahim and their baby, she wept on seeing the life disappear from his eyes. The old guards, who had followed the bloody trail Jocelyn had left behind her, now burst into the chamber. Their mockery was more than she could bear, as was the devastation she felt when they snatched the baby from her arms and laughed at the dead form of Ibrahim. It was all too much for Jocelyn as she realised they would never have been able to share a life together. One of the guards picked up the golden goblet which had belonged to Ibrahim (a reward from one of his most famous battles as a gladiator), then taking both the goblet and their baby, the guards turned to leave the chamber just as Abraham returned.

Abraham was furious and condemned them for their callous behaviour, reminding them of Jocelyn's close relationship to Cleopatra and how they were no more than fools to mock such a tragedy, and then to try and take the dead child too, they were a disgrace to their unit. Abraham's anger over-flowed as he declared that Cleopatra's wrath would wreak revenge on them all and removing the dead child from their clutches he demanded they all leave immediately.

Kneeling to take Jocelyn in his arms, Abraham gave her

baby back to her and helped her to stand up, saying he would take care of Ibrahim's body. With Jocelyn leaning into him for support, Abraham then beckoned to his daughter who was standing in the doorway, having returned filled with remorse. As Simona entered the chamber, she fell at Jocelyn's feet and pleaded for forgiveness. However, despite her usually generous nature and whilst Simona's own grief was as apparent and as pained as Jocelyn herself already felt, she could not forgive the woman that had taken Ibrahim from her.

"No, I cannot forgive you, Simona. How can you ask me for forgiveness when you have taken everything from me? I loved Ibrahim and our baby too; how can I ever forgive you?"

Jocelyn was devastated, her heart was broken and as she cried, Abraham could bear it no longer; he understood that his daughter could never be forgiven and he understood that it was likely she would be stoned to death for such a crime. With a heavy heart, Abraham told his distraught daughter to leave right away, to run and to never come back, for she would never be allowed to live should she be found. Helping Jocelyn back to her quarters, the honourable Abraham sent word for Cleopatra to be told of what had happened.

Kellie was crying in her sleep, sobs racked her body as she could no longer bear the tormented pain which was pulling her down into a blackness that she dared not enter. Crying out for help as she tried to stop herself being pulled down, Kellie subconsciously reached out her hand and someone, something, pulled her out.

Having been snatched out of her dream so vividly, Kellie was momentarily disorientated. Her face still wet from the tears she had cried, a sense of utter devastation lingered in her heart and mind, as she tried to make sense of what had just happened. Kellie got up out of bed and quickly wrapping her gown around her, she walked to the doors and pushed them open; she needed fresh air and to stay awake, she couldn't bear to slip back into that dream again. What had happened to her? Where had she been? Who were Jocelyn and Ibrahim? Kellie felt so sad it was like she was grieving herself; she had to tell Tom, it must be the goblet, there must be a link. What else could it be? Crazy thoughts scampered through her mind, as Kellie felt a combination of intense sadness, excitement and anticipation, whilst very scared all at the same time. Her mind was confused and she needed to escape from the dream.

As the reality of her real surroundings sank in, Kellie felt relieved and comforted to be standing on the veranda of her little house; she was safe and there was nothing to be afraid of. As she stood there remembering her dream, Kellie wondered about Jocelyn and Ibrahim in the distant lands of ancient Egypt and what would have happened, had Simona not been there, or if the baby Mary had survived. Kellie also pondered on how strange it was that she had always held a fascination for Egyptian history. Now, with the goblet turning up and them being able to keep it, surely it could only be this that had triggered her dream? The whole scenario was so uncanny that it felt almost surreal to Kellie. She must tell Tom, just to check she wasn't going crazy and that her imagination wasn't playing tricks with her mind.

After looking at the time and realising it was much later in the day than she had expected it to be, Kellie abandoned her plans of lying out in the sun; there was no way she could concentrate on reading a book right now anyway. But still needing to clear her head, calm down and think things through more rationally, she decided to spend some time outside, trying to do something normal before she told Tom.

As Kellie pottered around, tidying up her front garden and cutting back two plants which had decided to attempt a take-over of the lawn, she mulled over the dream. Apart from the vivid recall, which in itself was pretty unusual, Kellie also felt strangely different, yet she couldn't quite put her finger on why. It was like she knew something more, as if there were details which wouldn't quite come to the front of her mind just yet. This sense puzzled her, but no longer scared her. Sure, she had felt a little afraid when she first woke up, but in the hours which had passed since that moment, Kellie had calmed down again and was feeling much more relaxed. So much so, that she decided not to disturb Tom today and to think it all through again. Mostly this was because she wanted to relay the story to Tom accurately and calmly, instead of seeming like some neurotic woman who had lost her mind during the previous night. Which, if she was honest, was kind of what she had felt like just a few hours ago.

The rest of the day passed uneventfully as Kellie managed to finish off all the chores she had originally planned to do. Now feeling almost normal again, she flicked on the TV, hoping it would be more of a distraction in holding at bay any thoughts and memories from the dream, which threatened her planned evening of relaxation. But in spite of the TV, as the evening wore on and the night closed in, Kellie began to feel a little nervous about sleeping again. What if she went back into the dream? After worrying about it for longer than was good for her, Kellie decided that even if she did fall back into the dream, at least she would know what happened to Jocelyn after Ibrahim was killed.

Poor Jocelyn, Kellie reflected on how the pain of her grief must have totally consumed Jocelyn after losing both her lover and her baby. Even though, Kellie was sure, Cleopatra was bound to have looked after her and made sure she was protected, how could the bereaved Jocelyn have continued to live without Ibrahim and their baby? Kellie wondered how Jocelyn would have managed to survive that level of pain and devastation, or if it had driven her to take her own life. A sense of angst and anger grew within Kellie as she imagined the scene and what she would like to do to the guards who had snatched the baby away from Jocelyn. Wondering what Cleopatra might have done, she hoped justice had been served and that the guards had been severely punished for every moment of their cruel and callous behaviour. What about Simona, did she escape in time?

Kellie's imagination was beginning to run riot, so she flicked the TV over to another channel to watch something happy and bubbly, hoping it would distract her wandering thoughts away from those ancient times. But Kellie's dream recall was so strong that it was starting to feel like it was her own real past. She shook her head to try and dismiss her thoughts and got up to make herself some hot chocolate. That would do it, now feeling defiant, she hoped that sipping the creamy chocolaty liquid would drag her back to the reality of being in the present. After all, there would have been no hot chocolate in ancient Egypt!

Chapter 4

The Storm

It was morning again and after worrying herself silly the night before, Kellie awoke from her dreamless sleep feeling totally refreshed and very relieved. Flicking on the radio she listened to the news and weather forecast whilst getting ready for work. It didn't sound good and looking out of the window, Kellie could see grey clouds already rolling across the sky from outside of their normally sunny bay. Thinking how strange it was to see such an unusually dark and cloudy sky for this time of year, Kellie felt a tug of concern as she locked up and pushed her bicycle out onto the path, but then deciding she was being paranoid, she set off to the store to see Tom.

Already hard at it when Kellie arrived, Tom had almost completed his statuettes from the previous evening and was just putting the finishing touches to them before the store opened. Luckily, he needed far less sleep than Kellie (or even most regular people), so working longer hours really didn't bother Tom and suited his sleeping pattern perfectly, although very occasionally, he would have a blip and over-sleep, as he had done on Saturday. Tom was a hard worker, which greatly impressed his Great-Aunt Lilly and was why she had felt extremely comfortable to leave her precious store in Tom's more than capable hands.

Kellie rushed in through the back door, almost colliding with Tom as he was moving the goblet from the safe, over to its usual pride-of-place spot in their work-room. Tom side-stepped sufficiently as he greeted his dearest friend, "Morning, Kel, how was your Sunday? Did you manage to sort the garden out?"

"Hey, Tom. Yes thanks, all sorted. I even cut the grass,

so it's looking great out the front again. How was your day?"

"Oh, fairly uneventful, I was here working for most of it."

"So I see. You managed to finish the statuette then. Mrs Collins will be absolutely thrilled. It looks totally amazing, Tom, you're so clever!"

Picking up and closely studying Tom's work, Kellie was proud of what he achieved with his wood-working skills and was always impressed by the items he created and mended. Feeling privileged just to know him, as they shared this incredible life together, by her reckoning, their life really was perfect.

As Kellie chatted to Tom about everything, including the dodgy weather it looked like they were about to be hit with, she glanced at the goblet and wondered how to start relaying the story from her dream to Tom. But just as she was about to launch into her explanation, the bell on the front door tinkled as Mrs Terry entered the store. It was very early for her to be out and about so Kellie and Tom both walked through to the front to greet her.

"Good morning, Mrs Terry. How lovely to see you again and how was the wedding?"

"Ah, Tom and Kellie, my dears, hello to you both too. Well it was just wonderful to see all of the family again and I was so pleased with my new brooch, it matched my jacket perfectly and really set it off for me. I have to say though, whilst I did have a nice time, I was so glad to get back home again. You know, I really don't cope well with the noise of big gatherings these days, even when they are my family, whom I love dearly." Mrs Terry smiled and winked at them both. "Anyway, I was just passing by, on my way to pick up some groceries before the town gets too busy with visitors, and thought I would just pop in to see if you could spare any time to look at these two broken brooches? Do you remember you suggested I bring them in?"

Kellie did remember and said so, "Why absolutely, Mrs Terry. I would love to have a look at them for you. I can start work on them this very week."

As she held out her hand to pass them over, Mrs Terry touched Kellie's own hand and a shudder ran up the older woman's spine. Her gaze caught Kellie's eye and she quickly glanced at Tom, who was distracted by a lamp that had been knocked over across the store.

"You've had the dream haven't you?" she spoke quietly to Kellie. "I can tell. It's your time now." As Kellie looked a little puzzled at how Mrs Terry knew about her dream, the old lady added a little more loudly, "Do come and see me when the brooches are ready would you, Kellie? I have something to show you."

With that, Mrs Terry completely changed the subject and wishing them both a good day, she turned to leave and go about her usual business. Tom held open the door and said for his aunt's best friend to take good care of herself as she nodded, smiled and walked out, "Oh I will, Tom my boy, and you do the same too." Then, nodding at Kellie, she added, "Look after her; she's precious that one."

As Mrs Terry walked out, Tom was left puzzled as to what she had meant and looking at Kellie he asked the obvious question, "That all sounded very mysterious, and what dream was she talking about, Kel?"

"Ah, yes, well I was actually just about to tell you all about the dream when Mrs Terry walked in. It was really bizarre, Tom, and somehow, I really do believe, no, *I absolutely know* it has something to do with the Egyptian goblet we found."

Before she could say any more, the shop was suddenly filled with visitors; a coach party had arrived in town early and having taken a liking to the roadside appeal of their little store, many of them had made a beeline for it. This

45

meant that both Kellie and Tom were kept busy for the next couple of hours. Talk of the dream was forgotten whilst they sold quite a few items, happily relaying the history they knew about each piece. Even the old wardrobe trunk was snapped up by a smartly dressed lady who admired it greatly, telling them that it reminded her of her Great-Grandmother, who had loved to travel on the old steamers.

Due to the weight of the trunk, it had to be carried out to the coach by Tom and one of the gentlemen shoppers, who kindly offered to help him.

As the last customer left and the door-bell was silenced, Kellie looked at Tom, "Wow, what a busy morning, how great was that! I sure could do with a coffee. Do you fancy one?"

Picking up his latest wood carving, Tom grinned and nodded, "I will when I get back, Kel. I'm just going to pop across the road to deliver this little baby to Mrs Collins, she wants it today because it's Jim's birthday (Jim being her husband). Apparently, she's planning to leave the little fella sitting at the top of the stairs, so that when Jim goes upstairs after they've closed up shop, he'll see it waiting for him." Tom was laughing as he imagined the look of surprise on Jim Collins' face when he pulled open the door to go upstairs to the flat they shared above their store. Mrs Collins had told him she was calling the little wooden dog statuette Oscar, after a small dog that Jim's parents had adopted when he was a young boy.

Kellie called out her reply as she walked through to the back room to make the coffee and take a closer look at Mrs Terry's brooches, "Okay, no problem, I'll leave yours in the pot until you get back. I've no doubt Mrs Collins will keep you chatting for a while about little Oscar anyway."

The store felt strangely quiet after the rush of customers over the last couple of hours and with Tom gone too, Kellie felt a bit out of sorts. As she waited for the coffee to brew she was distracted by the goblet. Picking it up again and holding it under the light, Kellie watched the light reflected by the black stones that adorned it. At that very moment, a male voice spoke loud and clear inside Kellie's head and she swayed slightly, as if in a trance.

"...praying for me, you were praying for me, but I was gone, I was dead already. I loved you, I will always love you. How can I live without you? You were precious to me. Simona told Abraham. He came, he saw, he left. But he didn't tell. She stabbed me. I didn't know why. I guess she loved me, but couldn't have me because I loved you. How can this be real? Feel me close to you, feel me touch you..."

The voice suddenly stopped. Kellie was shocked, who was that? What was that? Now standing completely still and listening hard, she wasn't sure if the voice had been inside her head or spoken out loud, but either way, she was strangely unafraid, although also not able to move. Despite the shocked surprise at what had just happened to her, Kellie was acutely aware of her surroundings and could hear a dog barking outside as she spoke softly, "I know you are here, the dog is barking. He can sense you, I can sense you, how is that possible? How can the dog tell?"

Kellie continued to listen as the voice of Ibrahim spoke to her again. She tried to make sense of his words and the story they told. But it made her sad again and a small tear escaped and rolled down her face as Ibrahim spoke once more.

"Time stood still. The pain started in my stomach, it ripped open my torso. I was killed by a woman. I was killed for spite. They laughed. She laughed. The guards didn't care, they just laughed. Black Diamonds! I wanted to marry you. You were mine. How did they know? We tried so hard to be careful. I was your guard, you were my *dream. I loved you so. But we were not meant to be, they saw to that. Now you have someone big and strong to protect you. I sent him, he is a good man. This story, it is our story. You must tell it. You and he must stay together. You will be happy and he will look after you when it matters most. He will protect you. I know this, because I trained him well. He wasn't academic, but he was loyal and true, always true. It's time for me to go now. I will be back. Don't cry. Always smile. I love your smile, my love."*

Kellie swayed again, as the trance left her and she stood staring at the goblet, trying to make sense of what had just happened to her. Tom, she needed Tom, she had to tell Tom. Kellie called out his name and as if by some kind of psychic command, co-incidentally, Tom walked through the door at the front of their store, calling out to her, so that Kellie would know it was him. As he walked on through to the back, Kellie was still standing up and holding the goblet, but her face was now ashen. Tom could see something wasn't right and quickly took the goblet from her, setting it down as he pulled her into his arms and held her tightly.

"Whatever is it, Kel? What happened? Are you OK, my love?"

Tom was worried and hadn't even realised he'd used the words *my love*, but oddly, in that very same moment he realised, and there was no doubt in his mind, that actually he did love this woman, more than she would ever know. But, Tom also realised that he could never tell her, fearing the loss of their friendship if she should reject his love and leave Rosada Beachtown for good. If that happened, Tom knew it would hurt him so much more than suffering the pain of keeping his feelings of love for Kellie a secret.

Sitting Kellie down, Tom poured her a glass of water. Looking at him through shining eyes, Kellie thanked him and in a hushed voice she tried to explain, "Oh, Tom, you won't believe what just happened, the goblet, it..."

"Hush now, Kel, tell me later, you look like you're about to faint or something. Try and drink some water. Are you feeling OK?" Tom's voice was full of concern for Kellie. There was definitely something different about her that he'd not seen before. Yet even in this moment of looking slightly unwell, Kellie had never looked so perfect or so beautiful to him.

Kellie was shaken up more than she realised and as she looked at Tom with eyes that knew a secret, the desire to tell him burned into her mind once again. But just as she was about to speak, she was again interrupted, this time by a long low growl of what the two of them thought was thunder. The door to the store suddenly blew open and a huge gust of wind swept through the store so fast that it made Tom step out into the street to investigate. Looking down to where the beach was, he saw the sky was turning dark, as purple-grey clouds moved rapidly across the sea and whipped up the water into a huge twister. Running back inside, Tom had no idea of what to do; he'd never experienced a twister before, but he knew they didn't have time to run. There was no cellar or basement in their store, so he and Kellie retreated to the back room and waited as the noise of the storm grew stronger. People could be heard calling out and screaming as they ran for shelter against the strong winds, now battering their little town.

As the noise of the wind increased rapidly, Tom reached for Kellie and held her in his arms, both of them shocked at the suddenness of this totally unexpected and very scary event. Their own safety didn't occur to them as they silently prayed for their store to be spared from any damage, until a loud, but low-pitched, boom made them both jump and cling tighter to each other. Outside, the streets were quickly clearing of people as the wind forced everyone to seek shelter in the nearest building, realising there was a twister on its way and hoping the horrific wind would pass through their town without harming anyone.

As the twister grew in strength and speed, it weaved from side to side. A huge dust cloud was swirling with it, as small pieces of debris were flung out, randomly hitting cars and windows. Doors were banging loudly and breaking glass could be heard falling, as everyone feared the seriousness of this terrifying wind-storm. Panicked screams of fear rang out as the main body of the twister tore through their town. Water was being spun out of it, drenching everything it touched. The twister choked and roared its way up the whole length of Long Street, wrecking everything in its path as it smashed its way through their beach-side town. Branches that the twister had ripped from nearby trees were now being thrown through already broken windows by the rip-tide wind. Cars moved without warning, bashing into whatever stood in their way. The force of the wind was making the buildings shake violently, as possessions and shop goods fell to the floors. Some broke as they met the ground, others injured the people sheltering inside the shops and houses, which lined the whole street. Nobody knew what to do. Should they try to run or stay inside? What was best? Nobody knew, because their town had never experienced a twister before. Thankfully everyone stayed inside, thereby massively reducing the risk of injury and potential death-toll.

As the two friends clung to each other, Kellie cried out and Tom wrapped himself around her as much as he could, pulling her even closer to him to protect her, his beloved Kellie. Standing in the doorway, they each hoped the strength of the beam above it would offer some protection.

Unbeknown to them, stores were being wrecked all the way along the street as the wind tore through, ripping up boards and pulling shutters from the windows, flinging debris everywhere.

Tom dared to turn his head and look out towards the street, only to see a small car being carried in the wind funnel, and just at that very point, the roaring twister spat the car out towards them. As it came crashing into their store, Kellie screamed and Tom flung her away from him, seconds before the car struck his back and wedged itself in the doorway. The force of the car striking him catapulted Tom forwards and he crashed across their massive work bench, smashing his head against the wall. Kellie had fallen down and was screaming Tom's name, but he didn't respond. Desperate to help him, but unable to move due to the force of wind and the rubble showering over them both, Kellie could only lay where she fell, her arms covering her face and head, trying to protect herself. Larger pieces of wood, sticks and stones flew into their store and mixed with the falling rubble as Kellie felt something sharp dig into her leg; screaming out in pain, she then passed out.

The falling of the dust, twigs, stones and what was left of the wall in their store, slowed down as the twister rushed past, uncaring of the damage it had caused and taking the wind with it, as it continued on a destructive journey out of town.

Kellie came to and called out. There was fear in her voice, which was also shaking with shock, "Tom! Tom! Can you hear me? Tom! Are you OK? Oh God, Tom!"

Kellie was shouting and panicking, but Tom wasn't responding, and she had to free herself. Kellie could just about move enough to push away the debris that was covering her, but she struggled to free her right leg. Blood was running down her arm from a gash across her shoulder and a large shaft of wood was sticking out of her thigh, which was now bleeding profusely.

"Tom, Tom, oh my God, Tom, are you OK?"

Kellie was screaming now, but still there was no response from Tom. Fighting desperately to free herself and to reach Tom, Kellie was crying and panicking at the thought of him being seriously hurt. Then, finding a strength she didn't know she had, Kellie managed to push away the huge lump of debris trapping her leg.

Part of the wall which had collapsed as the car crashed into Tom, was what had covered them both. Some of the larger pieces had fallen onto Tom too. He lay silent. Covered in dust, with blood trickling from a serious wound to his head, Tom looked dead to Kellie and she screamed a wailing sound that could be heard down the street.

Outside it was mayhem, people were stumbling around, crying and nursing bleeding wounds, as they made their way back out into the street. Seeing the devastation around them, they were trying to come to terms with what had just happened to their lovely little town. Rosada Beach-town, which had until today, been a peaceful and uneventful place, where visitors came for their summer holidays.

Looking dusty and bedraggled, the residents and store owners were shocked and stunned, their eyes searching the damaged buildings and crying at what they saw. Whilst feeling thankful to be alive, they were also devastated at what they had lost amid the destruction that had changed their little town, in what had been no more than a matter of moments.

Nowhere in Long Street seemed to have been spared; all of the buildings had some kind of damage, some were a lot worse than others and some were like Tom and Kellie's store, ripped open, baring what remained of their destroyed contents for all to see. Nobody in the town had ever experienced a twister before. They knew they had been lucky until now. But here and now, in this very moment, they knew only too well the devastating effect of what nature could do, as it surely had proved, by destroying their beautiful little town. Help would come, but for now, it was up to them all to help each other.

Tom was unconscious and his pulse very faint. Despite Kellie's pleading for him to open his eyes, she was unable to wake him. In that desperate few minutes, as their lives had been turned upside-down, Kellie called out for help and began lifting some of the debris off of Tom, praying he would stay alive. Living a life without Tom was just too unbearable for Kellie and she cried as she struggled to free him. Trying to calm the panic within her as she again checked his pulse, Kellie could barely feel one and although Tom was still breathing, she knew it was too shallow. Panic took over. Kellie had to get help and quick!

Kellie climbed over the crashed car and somehow made her way through the wrecked contents of what was left of their store; her aim was to reach the street and see if anyone could help her to rescue Tom. Distant sirens could now be heard, help was on its way, but it wasn't close enough yet. A huge sense of relief passed over Kellie on hearing the sirens, but as she climbed out of the ruins, she saw just how bad the rest of the town was and couldn't believe that any of them had even survived.

Kellie staggered across the street to where the Collins family were huddled together, sitting on the remains of the boarded walkway which had previously run the length of their store. Holding onto her thigh to support the large wooden shaft which was still stuck in her wound, Kellie tried to relieve the jarring she felt at every painful step, as she half dragged her injured leg, trying to cross the street towards her neighbours. The badly seeping wound had soaked her clothes bright red. But she knew she needed to get help for Tom.

Kellie had almost reached the shocked family, before Jim Collins looked up and saw her. Jumping up, he rushed over to grab hold of her, supporting her weight as his wife joined him to help carry Kellie. Their little family were lucky; they had suffered no injuries themselves, but they did have a badly damaged home and business. Martha and Jim knew Kellie and Tom well and were keen to help, but despite her protestations, both of them insisted that Kellie needed to lie down to prevent further and serious loss of blood. They were only able to persuade her, by telling her that she would be no good to Tom like this. Martha tended to Kellie's leg, with the help of their daughter Maria, as both Jim and their teenage son, Nathan, stumbled across the street to help Tom.

Jim looked down the street as they crossed it. He could see people appearing – lots of people – carrying all kinds of equipment, clean blankets and bottles of what he assumed was water. It seemed like the rest of the local townsfolk had heard and seen the twister and whilst they and their homes had been unaffected, they'd realised the main shopping street of their little town had borne the brunt of the destruction and devastation. Each person, without a thought for themselves, had rushed to help their community, as workplaces ground to a halt and everyone stepped up to lend a hand. Not that much asking was needed, the small-town community was a strong one and the people there had always helped each other, so it was everyone's first instinct to down tools and go and help. Never before was that needed as much as it was today.

Several men walked up to join Jim and Nathan. Clearing the rest of the debris from Tom's legs, they managed to carefully move him out into the street. Someone had applied pressure to his head wound, as another passed over a bottle of water to clean the dust away so they could see how bad it was and dress it as best they could with a pad and piece of gauze from a medical kit. Thankfully some of the towns-people had returned to their homes and brought back first-aid boxes;

others had run back for towels to help dress the many wounds, until their injured friends, families and neighbours could be ferried to hospital for proper medical treatment. There were so many casualties, some of whom were walking wounded. Others had suffered broken bones. But worse still, some lay buried under the rubble of what had once been their stores and homes.

Tom was still unconscious, but now lying beside Kellie, who was holding his hand and talking to him as tears rolled down her dust covered cheeks, she again encouraged Tom to wake up. Pale and unresponsive, Tom's pulse was growing weaker. It didn't look good. Martha's heart went out to these two young people, who had known each other since childhood and who had become the very best of friends. Both of them were much loved by their neighbours and friends and Martha knew that Kellie would be heartbroken if Tom didn't make it; she reached out to touch Kellie's hand, trying to comfort her.

Due to the size of the town, the emergency services were very limited with only a few people employed in each service. The Police Chief and Fire Officer organised search and rescue parties, thankful for the many volunteers from their community. The phone lines were down in this part of town. So, with only the official two-way radios available, it was agreed that each team would have a walking reporter to check back with the nominated co-ordinator and advise who had been found and from which building.

Before long it seemed like virtually the whole of the town's population had descended upon Long Street and were now sifting through rubble and broken buildings, calling out names and carrying injured people out into the street. A couple of doctors triaged the wounded, prioritising who needed moving first, whilst instructing others on dressing wounds and applying pressure to stem severe bleeds. With only two ambulances and the nearest hospital forty miles away, it would be a slow process to move the injured until more help arrived from outside of town. Long Street itself was not drivable due to the amount of debris left behind by the twister, but luckily the other roads around the town were not so bad. Rescuers carried the injured to the next street on makeshift stretchers, most of which were doors that had been ripped from their hinges by the twister. The Police Chief commandeered all visible flat-bed pick-up trucks to ferry the walking wounded to the hospital.

By the time one of the ambulances arrived for Tom and Kellie, the two friends were in need of urgent help. Kellie's blood loss had been significant and despite Martha's valiant efforts to stem the flow, the extensive damage to her leg would need surgery to repair it. As the paramedics loaded Kellie onto a stretcher, she whispered a faint thank you to Martha and Jim, not knowing if they could hear her as she slowly drifted in and out, heading towards unconsciousness herself.

In the ambulance, both Tom and Kellie lay side by side. Tom was still unconscious, having not come around at all. Struggling with her own pain, but with fluids now being pumped into her, Kellie managed to reach across to hold his hand. The paramedics had done all they could and were now driving the two of them to hospital as fast as the ambulance would allow. Tom's breathing was shallow and Kellie sensed she was losing him. Unable to control her tears, Kellie cried as she told Tom that she loved him and would never forget him. And as Tom breathed his last breath, thoughts of Lilly entered Kellie's head. Instinctively, she knew that Tom's beloved aunt had been waiting for her precious boy and had finally come to take him home. Tom's hand was the last part of him that Kellie touched as she accepted he was gone from her forever, her heart breaking with every sob.

Martha was right, Kellie was indeed broken. Tom had surely saved her life when he'd pushed her away as the car had struck his back and catapulted him towards the wall. But now he was gone, snatched from his own darling Kellie, in a twisted turn of fate.

As Kellie finally lost consciousness, the paramedic began working on her again, desperate not to lose both of these young people.

Chapter 5

Loss, Bravery and Realisation

Kellie's head felt fuzzy and not quite right. Where was she? Trying to guess where she was and unable to fully open her eyes, she began listening carefully and could just about hear her parents' voices, but they were so low that she couldn't make out what they were saying. Kellie felt confused; the bed was strange, but as consciousness returned, she remembered the twister and Tom. Kellie cried as she whispered his name. On hearing her sob as her tears flowed freely, Kellie's parents broke off their conversation with the doctor and the three of them rushed back to her bedside. Holding Kellie's hand as she spoke, Barbara tried to reassure her weeping daughter.

"Hush now, my darling, you must rest. The doctors have repaired your leg; you were so very lucky, my love, there wasn't too much damage."

"But Tom…" Fresh hot tears ran down Kellie's face.

"We know, my darling, the doctor told us, we are so very sorry. Tom was such a lovely boy. We really can't believe that he's gone. It truly is beyond awful."

It was Kellie's father, Paul, who spoke this time; both he and Barbara had been shocked and horrified at the news of Tom's death. The two of them had thought the world of Tom and it had been because of his fine character that they had been less worried about Kellie moving out of the city and into *Jack's Place.* Having known him since he was a small boy, they had watched Tom grow into a fine man and now that very same man had given his life to save that of their own precious daughter.

Kellie's father would hold that debt of gratitude to Tom until his own life ended.

Tom was such a wonderful person and had always

been a true and good friend to their daughter, that both Paul and Barbara agreed and acknowledged, such a decent man was a rare find. They also told Kellie how they would *all* miss him terribly. Both of them knew only too well, how utterly devastated their precious and only daughter was and they were rightly worried about her and how she would cope with losing her beloved Tom.

Paul had to speak: "Tom was a brave man, Kellie. He saved your life by putting his own at risk and for that we will be forever grateful to him." Both Kellie's parents nodded in agreement as they comforted their daughter.

"But why did he have to die? We had such a nice life together and we've been friends forever. Why did he have to die? I loved him so much, what will I do without him?" Kellie's distraught questions tore into her parents' hearts like hot wires, their pain at seeing their only daughter so devastated, was almost too much to bear. They really didn't know what to say to bring her the comfort they knew she needed; it was the doctor who stepped in to answer Kellie's burning questions.

"Kellie, sometimes the people we love most are taken from us in the worst of circumstances. We always question *the why* and *what if*, but there are no answers that will ease your pain. The only thing you can do is to honour Tom's memory and be proud to have known him. Be thankful for the brief time he shared your life and know that he will be proud to have also shared his with you."

Kellie looked at the doctor and his kind eyes; she nodded in agreement, unable to speak, but wanting to acknowledge his thoughtful words. Her parents also looked at the doctor and nodded their understanding, relieved that he seemed to have found exactly the right words at just the right moment. They noted how Kellie seemed to visibly calm down as she closed her eyes again, Tom's whispered name lingering on her lips.

A member of the nursing team entered the room to check on Kellie and take note of the usual observations following surgery: blood pressure, heart rate, level of consciousness and movement. As the young nurse carried on with her work, the doctor indicated to Kellie's parents that he would like to speak to them and suggested that maybe outside would be best, whilst Kellie's observations were being performed. The fact was that the arrival of his nurse had offered the doctor an ideal opportunity to pull Kellie's parents away for a moment and so he took full advantage of the convenience of the interruption. Standing in the corridor facing Barbara and Paul, the doctor offered them his professional advice in the kindest way he could.

"It might be best to let Kellie rest for now. She will likely be sleeping again soon, because the anaesthetic takes time to wear off and with the shock she has had, her mind will also be exhausted. We can call you if there are any problems, but I would suggest you both go home and get some rest yourselves. Provided all is well overnight, I would expect Kellie to be allowed home in a couple of days, once she has seen the physiotherapist."

The doctor was gentle and caring as he spoke to Kellie's parents and thankfully, they accepted his advice, hoping that he would be right and that they could take Kellie home with them soon. Bidding the doctor farewell, Paul and Barbara thanked him again and after looking in to say goodbye to Kellie, they left for their own home.

Barbara's plan was to bring Kellie back to their family home, so that she could look after her daughter for a few more days. Of course, they'd not changed her bedroom since she had moved out, so it was still just as Kellie had left it and as far as Barbara was concerned, it was no trouble for them to have her come and stay.

Both Paul and Barbara were equally worried about their only child, wondering what she would do without

Tom and how she would cope.

Exhausted from crying and still recovering from her surgery, sleep overwhelmed Kellie's mind and her dreams returned. Only this time Tom was there, he was holding the goblet and saying he wanted her to have it, to have everything and to never forget him, for he would return one day, in another guise, in another body. Tom also told her that he loved her and as Kellie told him she loved him too, he smiled his broadest smile and blew her a kiss before fading into the ether. Even in her sleep, Kellie cried for Tom. Why did he have to go? Why couldn't he stay? Those questions played on her mind until the early morning sun streamed through the window and woke her up.

Kellie wanted to leave, she had to get out of the hospital and go back to where she had last seen Tom, before the storm. As expected, Kellie wanted to go back to what had been normal life for them, before the twister had ripped through their lives and homes. But of course, that life had gone and it would never be the same again, which was something Kellie was yet to come to terms with.

Paul and Barbara showed up at visiting time as promised, hoping that Kellie would indeed be allowed home with them. Thankfully, her wound looked good and the doctor said that as long as Kellie rested for the next couple of days and had someone with her to help her wash, dress and to cook for her, she should be fine to go home. They assured the doctor, they would take care of her and after agreeing to bring her back to see the Physiotherapist in a few days, the doctor signed Kellie's discharge papers.

Both Paul and Barbara knew Kellie would probably want to go straight back to Rosada Beachtown, but they had yet to drive down and see what was left of it. They had agreed that, as planned, Barbara would take Kellie home for two more days, whilst Paul drove down to the beach to check out the damage and see what, if anything, was left of Kellie's little house. Paul would also check on Tom's store and report back, suggesting Barbara could then bring Kellie down in a few days to at least have a look, even if she couldn't stay there.

That was their plan and it was a sensible one. But as expected, Kellie protested, so Paul took charge and said that as her father, she should let him take care of things, just until she could get back on her feet. Which he also informed Kellie, would literally only be possible after she had completely rested for the minimum two days the doctor had advised, before seeing the Physiotherapist again. Knowing her parents were right jarred with Kellie, because she knew it also meant waiting even longer to go back to Rosada Beachtown, which was her home now and where she had been so happy living and working alongside Tom. Kellie desperately needed to see what was left of her life there.

The two days of rest came hard because she was used to being so active but, as the doctor had predicted, Kellie's leg needed some time to heal and if the truth were known, she was still feeling a little wiped out from the trauma of it all. Lots of sleep was more the order of the day and despite her obvious reluctance and fear of falling back into sad dreams, Kellie's tiredness eventually overwhelmed her and she slept for hours during the daytime, on both days, as well as throughout each night.

Barbara was relieved that they'd managed to persuade Kellie to stay in the city, but like her husband, she also dreaded what Rosada Beachtown might look like now. After hearing how the twister had wound in from the sea, Barbara and Paul both felt sure that *Jack's Place*, was likely to have been completely flattened and if that was indeed the case, they knew Kellie would be devastated. Barbara shuddered, that moment loomed ahead of them like a black cloud and she was understandably worried at how her daughter would deal with such news.

Paul telephoned them around tea-time and explained how badly the main street in town had been torn apart and that Tom's store would indeed need extreme renovation, if not re-building. Most of its contents had been ripped away by the tearing winds which accompanied the twister, but he told them he'd been able to rescue a few bits and pieces, which were now stowed in the back of his truck. Paul said the only thing of any possible value had been a gold coloured goblet, which he'd found covered in dust on the floor in front of where the crashed car had been. Thankfully the car had since been removed by the fire teams. Even the counter which had displayed the jewellery, had been smashed to smithereens and would need careful picking over of the broken glass, to retrieve any of the trinkets it had previously held. Other than that, he added that only the old safe was still standing in its rightful place, but that it was locked. Kellie gave Paul the combination so he could rescue its contents.

The better news was that remarkably, Kellie's own house, *Jack's Place*, was virtually untouched. Apart from the table and chairs that used to be on the veranda, which seemed to have been whipped away by the wind, Paul assured them there were only small pieces of debris scattered across the garden. Otherwise the house was safe and no windows had been broken. Paul himself could hardly believe it, having seen how bad the town was. It seemed the twister had virtually taken a straight-line right through the main shopping street of town, leaving the surrounding residential areas virtually untouched. Which was probably just as well, because the emergency services reckoned there would have been far more fatalities, had it hit more of the town's timber built homes. Barbara was relieved about *Jack's Place* and hugged Kellie at hearing the news. Kellie couldn't believe that her little house had been saved and although she too felt relieved, she would have lost it in an instant if it meant Tom could still be there.

Knowing that Tom kept his ledgers and important papers in the safe – which was still stood in the back-room of the store – was a relief to Kellie, for she knew they would include the insurance documents. Which also meant Paul and Kellie could at least let the insurers know and start the ball rolling with regard to demolition and/or repairs. The safe also contained a few random items of value, although no significant jewels, other than the two brooches belonging to Mrs Terry; Kellie had no idea of how valuable the brooches were and realised she would need to find Mrs Terry to return them to her. What intrigued Kellie most was the goblet and how strange it was that it had survived yet again and with no apparent damage. Unlike Tom, she thought, who had been fatally damaged by the car that had struck him. Fresh tears sprang into Kellie's eyes and she cried for Tom again. Barbara hugged her daughter, wanting to take away the pain, but knowing she could not. All she could do was to comfort Kellie each time her grief for Tom overwhelmed her emotions.

After two days, Paul agreed that Barbara should drive Kellie down to the beach, so she could see the damage for herself and begin to piece her life back together. The hospital had loaned Kellie some crutches to help her walk on her injured leg, but again, she was advised to take small steps and for not too long at any one time. Healing would take quite a few weeks, they said, possibly even months before she felt a hundred per cent again. Whilst knowing she had to listen to medical advice, Kellie also felt frustrated at not being able to help sort out the store and Tom's flat. It felt like that was the only thing that she was able to do for her dearest friend, the man who had given his life to protect her. Yet, here she was, not even fit enough to go and do that for him.

Taking fresh food supplies and some bottled water with them, Barbara helped Kellie into their 4x4 and drove down to Rosada Beachtown. The roads were fairly clear until they got closer to the town, but overall the journey hadn't been bad and it wasn't too long before they arrived safely at Kellie's beach-house.

Paul had been using the sofa-bed to sleep on since he'd arrived, leaving Kellie's bed untouched. He'd also tidied up the front garden, so the house looked much the same as when Kellie had left it, minus the table and chairs from the veranda. But that was fine. Kellie knew how lucky she was to still have her house. Stepping inside, she drew in a deep breath, remembering the meal that she and Tom had shared on the veranda just two days before the storm. Barbara could sense her daughter's emotions and just as a mother often does, swung into organising mode, sorting out the groceries they'd brought and then settling them into the house, before she took Kellie up to look at Tom's store, or what was left of it.

As Kellie and Barbara's car pulled up outside the store, Paul heard their arrival and looked up, waving at them as he stepped out of the debris. Walking over to them, he hugged and kissed both his wife and his daughter.

Martha had also heard them arrive and called out to let Jim know, as she also crossed the road to see Kellie. Relieved to hear that young Kellie was back, Jim ran across to his wife as they each hugged their friend and neighbour, and told her of their sadness at losing Tom. The three of them had shared something Barbara and Paul had not, the tragic experience of the twister and each of them feeling very thankful to be alive, they hugged again. As they broke the moment and stepped back, Kellie's mother said hello to Martha and Jim, as Barbara thanked the couple for everything they had done to help both Kellie and Tom. Each of them reiterating their sadness at the tragedy of losing Tom.

New friendships were born through the events of that devastating day, which had changed all of their lives. None of them would ever be the same again. The whole town had rallied round and people had offered spare rooms, as well as their own time to help clear, repair and re-build the town. Paul had been extremely grateful when two local teenagers had offered to help him clear up what was left of Tom's store and see what else they could salvage. Most of it had ended up in a huge pile on the road just in front of the store, waiting to be photographed, before then being taken away by the many trucks which had been provided by the state authorities.

Several insurance assessors had visited the town and were now working with the residents who needed their help. Luckily one of those assessors also worked for the insurance company that Tom had engaged, so he had been able to check and photograph the store before Kellie had arrived. Structural engineers had subsequently been called in to inspect and advise on what should be done in terms of repairs versus demolition for all of the buildings in Long Street. Looking at what was left of their store, Kellie hoped they could recover the majority of their building and just repair it rather than demolish it. Tom's flat above the store would also need to be sorted out, but they could not even venture into it until the structural engineers had been back to assess it for safety.

Kellie was in no rush to enter Tom's flat so the delay suited her; besides, at that moment in time, it seemed wrong to her to even be going in there when he was where he was – she still couldn't bring herself to say that Tom was dead. Kellie felt like she would be intruding into Tom's private space, even though she'd been in there a thousand times with him. But that was the thing, she had been *with* Tom and now it was just her and Tom was no longer around. It was wrong, so very wrong and so very unfair. Kellie began to wilt as Barbara touched her daughter's arm and suggested they check over the papers back at the beach-house, so that Paul and the boys could carry on. Kellie nodded and after thanking the boys and her father again, she turned away, tears brimming and barely under control as she slowly walked back to the car with her mother.

Because of the tragic events that had taken place, the people in the town had rallied round to help each other. All that help and support felt all the more precious to Kellie, knowing she had to continue her life without Tom. Back at the beach-house, Kellie reflected on how very lucky she was to live in this town, with such wonderful people and to have such strong, supportive parents. Voicing a *thank you* out loud, made Barbara look up from the papers she was reading.

"What was that, honey?"

"Oh, I was just thinking aloud, I'm so glad you and Dad are here to help me, I can't thank you both enough. Do you think we, I mean, the town, will ever recover?"

"Yes, honey, you and the town will; there are so many good people here, they will re-build Long Street and it will be better for it. People will be stronger and properties will be newer. It will help you all to make a fresh start," then touching Kellie's arm, Barbara continued, "and we're also glad we could be here for you, Kellie darling. We're just so thankful to Tom, his bravery in protecting you, means we actually still have you, our most precious daughter."

Kellie welled up; she was still so fragile when it came to talking about Tom, but she knew she had to be stronger and carry on. Tom would have wanted her to, of that Kellie was certain. As she tried to read her daughter's mind, Barbara broached an important question, "What do you think you will do with the store?"

"Well, it's not really my decision. I mean, it was Tom's place, not mine. I doubt I will have any say in what happens to it now. I suppose the insurance company will speak to the lawyers and sell it."

"But, well, ahmm, I'm guessing you haven't read through any of these papers then, sweetheart? Did you not know that Tom has added you as a co-owner?"

"What? Co-owner? When?" Kellie was shocked.

"Well it looks like it was very recently actually. I assumed you had spoken about it and just not told your father or me." Barbara now looked as puzzled as Kellie felt. Tom had never mentioned to Kellie that he was giving her joint ownership of his store, not once. This news came as a complete surprise to her.

"It seems our Tom must have loved and trusted you very much, Kellie, to want to share his business and his life with you. Here, have a look at these papers."

As Kellie scanned through the documents her mother had passed to her, she could almost hear Tom's voice in her head and it seemed to be saying... *I wanted this, Kellie. I wanted it for us and for us to be together always. I loved you more than words could ever say and I wish I had actually told you that myself.*

Feeling shocked at this news, Kellie asked her mother if she could check the wording again. But there was no need for checking, because it was all true. Tom, in his genuine and kind way, had realised that if anything were to ever happen to him, Kellie would be left without a job and with no other family to leave the business to, he knew she would be the best person to keep it going for both him and Great-Aunt Lilly.

But Tom's most important reason for making the change was that he had loved Kellie very much and could think of no one that he would rather share his business with, or leave it to, should anything ever happen to him.

Barbara was thrilled for Kellie, although she also

recognised how hard it would be for her daughter to continue the business without Tom. She was still not convinced that Kellie would have the strength to do that, not without having Tom there to share it with.

When Paul returned to the beach house, he was exhausted, covered head to foot in dust and most definitely in need of a long hot shower. Updating the two women in his life, Paul said that he and the boys had done as much as they possibly could and what they had been able to reasonably salvage, was now in the back of his truck. It wasn't much, but it would be something to start with. Paul had also brought in a cardboard box containing the contents of the jewellery cabinet and put it on the table. Having scooped it all out so that Kellie could work through the shattered glass to retrieve the actual jewellery. Whilst Paul went off to shower, Barbara offered to help Kellie and suggested they'd best use some gloves so they didn't cut their fingers. It would be a painstaking task, but they began carefully picking their way through the box.

The insurance assessor had told them not to try and shift any more debris until the structural engineers had finalised their inspection. The assessor had been concerned for their safety, but he also knew that under the circumstances, it was almost impossible for anyone to just leave everything to the open elements for days on end. Secretly, he expected Paul to still return, despite his advice and knowing he would probably do the same if he were in their shoes. Everyone in town who had been affected was doing exactly the same. All of them were desperate to get to a point of being able to move forward.

Half an hour later, Paul re-joined his wife and daughter. Now fresh from the shower and feeling very hungry, he suggested they finish off the jewellery tomorrow and take some time to eat. With food made, Paul now sat at the table with them as Kellie and Barbara proceeded to tell him what they had found in Tom's papers about Kellie already being a co-owner of the store. Like Kellie, Paul too was astounded and again sent up a silent thank you to Tom. What an amazing guy he had been and how much he would be missed by their little family. Life could be so cruel sometimes, but then just when you think all is lost, out of nowhere, someone offers you a helping hand. Such luck was not lost on Paul and he breathed a sigh of relief at knowing his daughter's future was safe, as he also raised a glass to Tom, to toast and thank their much-loved friend.

Exhausted from the day's events, the three of them decided an early night was needed and thankfully, they each slept solidly, with Paul and Barbara sharing the sofa-bed and Kellie in her own bed.

As the morning dawned and sunshine streamed into her little home by the sea, just for a very few moments, Kellie forgot about the twister and that Tom had been killed. But as the memory of the last few days returned again, she began to sob quietly. Hearing their daughter's sorrow awoke both Paul and Barbara, and as they both jumped out of bed to comfort her, they again thought on how tough life was going to be for their daughter whilst she was grieving for Tom. It was a long road ahead that she had to travel and they also knew that there was little they could do to help relieve that suffering, except to be there and to love and support her through the pain. But that brought little comfort to them personally, for they wanted to be able to do so much more and yet knew that they couldn't.

With little else to do now that they had to await the structural engineers, Kellie decided to assume responsibility for dealing with the insurance company, lawyers and the bank. She very much needed to keep busy and to start the process of re-building and recovering hers and Tom's business. Barbara and Paul said they would stay for a few more days to help her, which Kellie really appreciated. In between grieving for Tom, she would need to deal with responsibilities that she had no experience in and which would certainly challenge her resolve, so to have her parents there to lean on, should she need to, would be great. Kellie was already finding that there were all kinds of complications to deal with, arising from the fact that Tom had died. Not least of all, how would she be able to carry on without him, and did she even want to re-open the store? Lots of questions repeatedly ran through her tired mind.

Kellie's parents wisely advised her that she should continue with refurbishing the store for the time being, because that would give her a focus and a purpose to carry on. Besides which, they reminded her that Tom would be devastated if she were to just walk away from it. Kellie knew they were right and whilst she was struggling with her grief, she also recognised it would be a long and difficult road for her to recover from such a devastating loss. Tom had meant the world to her and she felt utterly lost without him, but was certain of one thing, Tom would want her to continue living and to make their shop her own.

Part 2

Chapter 6

New Beginnings

It was now thirteen months since the terrible day that Kellie had lost her dearest friend. It had been a day that she would never forget and one which was imprinted on her brain forever. Tom's brave sacrifice and his quick reactions had resulted in Kellie surviving the twister, which had destroyed their business and most cruelly, had taken Tom's life. Lucky to have escaped serious injury and apart from a dull ache which bothered her occasionally, Kellie's leg was now pretty well healed. Since being discharged from the hospital's care, she had followed the advice given by the physio team and exercised daily, mainly by cycling to her store.

The whole town, including Kellie herself, had been astounded at how quickly the insurers worked to re-build the heart of their community. For the residents, saying that they felt grateful didn't even come close to how they were feeling; the re-build was worth so much more to them than just that. Emotions were still raw for some and to have received such quick help and support had been instrumental in the recovery of their livelihoods and general well-being.

For Kellie, it felt very strange not having Tom around and she was still experiencing both good and bad days. But despite her sadness at losing Tom, having been supported so well by the people around her, Kellie had not felt as alone as she had expected to. In fact, much to her parents' relief, Kellie had actually managed to start moving forwards and was finally enjoying bits of her life again.

The store itself had been given a new look and feel to it which was something Kellie had needed to do. In part, that was because without Tom's repairing expertise and wood carvings, she had needed to think of new ideas in what to sell and how to go about changing their store. Re-naming it had been an important step forward and Kellie had chosen LTK Emporium, honouring Lilly and Tom, whilst including herself and modernising the appeal of the store to new customers. Kellie had decided she needed to bring in other ideas and talents, so she reserved a small section of the shop for local artists to display and sell their wares. This section had recently become quite successful and having discovered some very talented artists in their little town – potters, painters and jewellery makers to name a few – Kellie had felt encouraged to be more creative herself and had taken up patchwork quilting. This new skill had kept her very busy making small personalised quilts – mainly for babies' cots and children's beds – which she displayed next to the rack of new and of vintage clothing, both of which were proving to be popular additions to the store. In fact, Kellie's quilts had become so popular that she was struggling to keep up with demand.

All in all, the new store was becoming a little gold-mine and a regular stopping point for the visitors to their town. Even the newly added 'book-corner' was popular and had become almost like a small library. That suited Kellie perfectly, because she loved the company of the children and adults who popped in daily to use it, some of them often swapping old books they had read, for something new on the shelves and leaving a small donation for Kellie.

Not wanting to leave *Jack's Place*, Kellie had decided to rent out Tom's flat above the shop, which had added to her regular income. On the whole, she felt very lucky that all was working out as well as it was, which was thanks to Tom's undeniable generosity in sharing ownership of his and Lilly's store.

Mrs Terry had also been popping in every week, just to check on Kellie and to make sure she was coping OK; having not forgotten that before the twister had ripped into their town, she had needed to speak to Kellie about her dreams. But, with Tom gone and the devastation that both his loss and the twister had caused, Mrs Terry had felt that Kellie had needed more time to recover, before she could speak to her about those dreams.

Now that they were thirteen months on from that disastrous day, it seemed that the right time had now come; Mrs Terry popped in for that very special chat late one Saturday afternoon, just before Kellie was due to close up. The bell over the door tinkled as the older lady pushed it open and walked in.

"Good afternoon, Kellie my dear, how has business been this week?" Mrs Terry beamed a happy smile at her young friend.

"Oh, hello, Mrs Terry, how lovely to see you. Please do come in and browse if you want to." Kellie was always happy to see her favourite customer.

"Thank you, Kellie, but it's just a social call today, my dear, to see how you are and maybe have a little chat."

"Oh, that's so lovely of you and actually, I was just about to close up, so if you'd like to wait a few minutes, I could make us a pot of tea to share." Mrs Terry acknowledged that good idea, thankful of Kellie's generous nature. As she busied around the store, preparing it for closing, Kellie chattered on.

"I'm feeling very well actually, Mrs Terry, and as you will no doubt have noticed, the store is quite busy these days, what with all these new little sections." Kellie gestured to the book-corner and the quilts. "I feel very lucky actually, because it's been a bit of a bumper week. Although to be honest, I am really looking forward to having the day to myself tomorrow." Kellie grinned at her dear old friend and carried on: "So, I plan to just relax and do nothing. Well, maybe read the book I've been trying to get into for the past few weeks. How are you anyway, Mrs Terry? Have your headaches stopped yet?" Kellie had been worrying about her friend after hearing how she had been suffering from bad headaches for quite a few weeks, and being the strong, independent and down-right stubborn woman she was, Charlotte Terry had refused to see the doctor.

"Ah yes, thankfully they have and I'm just dandy thank you, Kellie, just dandy. I do have something to talk to you about though, so that cup of tea together would be perfect."

As Kellie popped into the back-room, Mrs Terry sat on the cushioned bench-seat which stood in the shop for Kellie's customers to use. It looked so inviting, having been carefully set together with a beautiful little side table and its matching chair. Looking around the much-improved store, Mrs Terry nodded with appreciation and whilst she was momentarily alone, she spoke softly to her old friend Lilly, knowing she was listening.

"Lilly my dear, you would be so proud of our girl; look what a delightful store she has created for you and Tom."

Mrs Terry had always been a great believer in the spirit world, having experienced many things across the years, including the messages she occasionally received for other people from their dear departed, and which often brought the receivers great comfort. It was a fact that Mrs Terry was absolutely convinced of, without any doubt whatsoever, that once our earthly body dies, our spiritual energy is released to roam free, existing and thriving in the ether that surrounds us all, residing alongside the spiritual energies of passed loved ones, some of whom still watch over the people they once knew and cared for during their lifetime on earth.

As Kellie returned to the front of the store, she was carrying a tray holding their pot of tea, with its matching milk jug, plus two very dainty tea-cups, all of which were set upon it so prettily. Kellie had included a favourite tea-plate, even though it didn't match any of the other china, upon which she had placed several of her delicious home-made oat-based cookies. With tea poured and both of them settled, as she looked around the store again, Mrs Terry complimented Kellie on her brilliance, adding how both Lilly and Tom would have been so proud of her. Kellie glowed at that thought and for a moment, her underlying sadness was replaced with pride and love, both for Lilly and Tom, as well as their little store and Mrs Terry herself. How lucky she was to know this wonderful lady who, over the years, had shared so many memories and funny stories, which Kellie often listened to and delighted in. The two women chatted about many different things, including how well the store was doing, the lovely sunny weather and Kellie's own home by the sea. Before they knew it, more than an hour had passed and Mrs Terry apologised for keeping Kellie so long.

"It really is no trouble, Mrs Terry, I so love our little chats and you always manage to bring Aunt Lilly and Tom close to me again." In truth, Kellie didn't want to let her go just yet, because of that very closeness that Charlotte Terry always seemed to bring to her.

"Well that's a blessing then, my dear. I know they would love that you feel their presence. You do know they are always looking out for you, don't you, Kellie? They watch over you to help you in whichever way they can. They are so very proud of you, my dear, proud beyond belief at how incredibly strong you have been and how you have worked so hard to turn the store around. I truly believe that you have nothing but exciting times and good experiences ahead of you now."

Kellie felt a little surprised at those words, but she was happy and relieved to hear such thoughts, smiling, she thanked her old friend.

"It's no trouble at all, Kellie. Now, I know you are aware of my beliefs and how I can communicate with our dear departed, but there is something else I do need to be able to tell you and it's very important, so I have to say it, do you mind?"

Not knowing what Mrs Terry was about to share, but also feeling intrigued, Kellie responded warmly, "Not at all, Mrs Terry, please do continue. I'd love to hear what you have to tell me." Kellie was a willing listener, for she too held similar beliefs to her friend. Although, until the goblet had first arrived, Kellie had been unaware of any personal spiritual abilities, other than the bizarre dreams which had invaded her sleep-time. But since the goblet had arrived, Kellie often wondered if, in those dreams, she had somehow managed to span the centuries back to ancient times. Always then quickly dismissing such ideas as fanciful thoughts, or her own vivid imagination.

Now though, Kellie wondered if she was right to have previously doubted herself, because every day since Tom had died, she had touched the golden goblet and said good morning to him. Now convinced that somehow, by carrying out that small gesture, had kept her connected to Tom, because every day, with every touch, Kellie had felt something powerful, yet she couldn't quite explain what it was she was feeling, or even what it meant.

Unaware of Kellie's thoughts, Mrs Terry continued with her story: "I always knew there was something special about you, Kellie, since the first time I met you all those years ago, when you were just seven years old. There was something about you that I could sense was *old*, like you were an *old soul*. I never really saw anything spectacular happen back then when you spent your summers here, but I knew there was something bubbling beneath the surface, which was meant to come out later in life.

"It was when you and Tom first showed me the goblet

that I realised what it was, because I had received a message for you. I knew it was for you, but I had to bide my time to tell you when the moment was right. Then the twister came and destroyed everything and that moment was lost. It's only now, today, that I feel I can pass this information on to you. Yes, it feels like the time is right."

Mrs Terry watched Kellie's reaction, then glancing towards the back-room of the store, to where the goblet stood in the young woman's work-room, Mrs Terry asked a question, "Do you think you could fetch the goblet please, Kellie, and place it on this table? I won't touch it. I just need it to be here with us. Close to us both."

"Of course, Mrs Terry, I'll just be a moment." Kellie was intrigued and got up to fetch the goblet, standing it carefully in the middle of the round table, before sitting down in the chair again and waiting for Mrs Terry to continue.

"Jocelyn, the name Jocelyn is being given to me; it is you, you are she, but you only remember parts of the story and I have to tell you what really happened."

Mrs Terry's look was suddenly distant, the words were coming, but it was as if someone else were telling the story. As Kellie listened, completely absorbed by what Mrs Terry was saying, the older woman's heart was beating a little faster as the words flowed once more into her mind, willing her to share them; her voice had changed and to an outsider, it would have been difficult to say for sure what had changed. But Kellie knew. Charlotte Terry now sounded like she was from ancient Egypt times. Her voice suddenly deepened.

"*Mary, our baby was Mary, but she died in childbirth. They knew she was mine, but I was black and you were white, so it was forbidden. Our lives were never meant to be together, don't you see, they would never have let us be together. The day they came, you ran to me to warn me and to protect me, but she was ahead of you. You always blamed yourself for giving me away, but you didn't know that it wasn't you. She told the guards, but not before she stabbed me. My blood was like red wine, there was a goblet on the floor, it was mine, they took it, but it will come back to you. Golden in colour, so you will know it when you see it. We both drank from it. It was our cup you said. You were wise, but blinded by our love, which was special, meaningful. The wine mixed with my blood as you held me and you cried as I died in your arms. You couldn't forgive, but you must find it in your heart to move on, to allow love to return and peace to reign. Peace and love must always be our message. People will say and do strange things that we wouldn't do, but we must forgive and heal them. If you can forgive, it will heal the wounds, she will then move on and let go of her resentment."*

Mrs Terry paused and Kellie sat staring at her, absorbing every word, amazed at the coincidence to her own dreams.

After glancing at the goblet again, Mrs Terry continued: *"Reach out again. Good must always prevail, you must always take the higher ground, that is the only way we lived our lives and how I died for you again, so you could live. I chose to go early. I knew I had to save you. I know it doesn't make sense now, but it will soon and you will know. You will realise that it was all meant to be repeated. Life will never be the same again, but it is precious, live it, love it, always. Remember I am always yours. Be sure of that, for my love will never fade. It will be with you throughout every lifetime on this earth. I will see you again, far away in the future. Meanwhile I will live every life with you and come to you again in later life, every time. For you need to grow and learn for yourself, before I can return each time, that is my restriction. But know I am with you and I will not let you fall further than you can cope with. You are strong, you always have been since that ancient time when we were one, joining our love for eternity."*

Mrs Terry paused.

Kellie's eyes filled with tears, her voice was hushed as she whispered one word, "Oh…" She was unable to say any more than that. Mrs Terry's words had resonated with her and she knew they were right, for her own dreams had told her as much, but that had been in bits and pieces and she had not been able to piece the whole story together, until now. The two women looked at each other and smiled. Something had passed between them and Mrs Terry looked relieved. Kellie sat for a moment and a puzzled look crossed her face, as she stared into the kind eyes now looking back at her. Shaking her head slightly, Kellie realised something and she really couldn't explain how or why, but she just *knew*.

"It's you…"

Kellie gasped a breath as Mrs Terry held hers, waiting for Kellie's next words, as the younger woman's mind tried to make sense of what was now flooding into it.

"Mrs Terry, it's you! Isn't it? Yes, you are Simona! But how? How is that even possible? Did you always know that we knew each other from ancient times?"

So many questions, that Kellie couldn't quite believe what was passing between them. The energy felt so strong it almost crackled and she now felt like they had known each other forever, but also that something had been left unsaid between them. Never before had she felt anything like it, not until this very moment.

Mrs Terry suddenly looked incredibly sad as she replied, "I believe it was me, Kellie, although I never knew for sure, not until the goblet came. When I first saw it, something inside me drew me back into ancient times. The goblet, and a dagger, both of them mean something. I cannot believe the story I have told you, but it is exactly as it was given to me, and I feel great sadness at what I have done in my past life, no, in *our* past life. I need your forgiveness. I am old and tired. I feel lonely without my friends, Kellie. I need to go, but I am being kept here. Can you forgive me, my dear? Please?"

Kellie was shaking slightly, but her instinct was strong as she replied, "Mrs Terry, there is nothing to forgive; you have always been so kind to me, how can I forgive something I no longer feel?"

With kind eyes and a gentle manner, Mrs Terry suddenly looked very frail as she explained, "It is I who feels the pain, Kellie my dear, you have been such a good soul that the pain has been kept from you. Ibrahim returns in every life until you can forgive me. I hope this time, in this life you can release us both and be free to love again for eternity."

Kellie could barely believe it: did Ibrahim really return in every lifetime? Now thinking back, she knew she had loved Tom, but had not been able to tell him before he was taken away from her. Was part of Ibrahim's soul inside of Tom? Is that why he had sacrificed his life for her too?

"Oh, Mrs Terry, we both need to move forward in our lives. I lost Tom and you have lost your friends. I realise now why you never found love again, but truly, I want you to love and to be loved. You are a good person, Mrs Terry, and someone I am very glad to have in my life, and not just right now, but ever since I first knew you."

Kellie suddenly felt like pieces of a lifelong puzzle were fitting together and she knew she had to say the words, even though to her, it felt like there was nothing to forgive. Mrs Terry sat with tears in her eyes as she waited and listened to Kellie, her hands clasped together, as she looked upon the younger woman's now smiling face.

"Mrs Terry, my dear Mrs Terry, in this life there is nothing to forgive you for. You have been a wonderful friend to both Tom and me, and of course to dear Aunt Lilly before us. But I know you need to hear these words and so for your past life, when you were Simona and I was the Lady Jocelyn, for the wrongs in *that* life, I truly do forgive you. Your pain and suffering since then has been for long enough. In this life, you have more than made up for that past wrong. It was a moment of madness and fear, of grieving for a love you could not have. It is past now and it was so very long ago. We can each move on with forgiveness in both our hearts, for I realise that I had held something from you too back then, which was the freedom to receive love from someone as special as Ibrahim."

The two women stood up and hugged each other for the longest time. As their energy joined together, a warmth filled the room and love like they had never before felt, surrounded them both in perfect serenity.

"You know, Kellie my dear, this has been one of the most cherished parts of my life, to have known you and Tom. Dearest Lilly was my most precious friend and I feel like you have been an extended family for her and for me too. Now I must get off home; please do keep your heart open to new possibilities, Kellie. You know, I've always thought it best to keep smiling, because you never know who is falling in love with your smile."

With that thought, Mrs Terry thanked Kellie once again for listening, for understanding and most importantly, for forgiving. Bidding the younger woman goodbye, she left to make her way back home.

As Charlotte Terry lay in her bed that night, she felt strangely free and smiled as she welcomed the love that filled the room; her dearest Lilly having appeared beside her, holding out both hands and smiling down at her oldest friend as she welcomed her into the spirit world once more.

Chapter 7

A Stranger in Town

As Kellie locked up the store that evening, she had a strong feeling that she would not be seeing Mrs Terry again and it was if their chat was also a real goodbye. Kellie knew Mrs Terry had wanted to be forgiven so she could move on herself, but she felt sad at saying goodbye. Pulling herself up short and realising where her thoughts were leading her, Kellie muttered to herself, "What on earth am I thinking? Of course I'll be seeing Mrs Terry again, she always pops in to say hello!"

Dismissing her thoughts as purely fallout from what the two women had experienced earlier, Kellie pushed her bike out into the road. The sun had long since gone down and darkness was beginning to fall. Placing her feet onto the pedals then regaining her balance, Kellie set off for home.

With nothing planned, other than an evening of relaxation before her day off, Kellie felt calmer than she had in months, in fact she was actually feeling quite happy as she cycled home. Yes, today had been a good day and Tom would have been proud of her, of that she felt sure. Making her way down Long Street, Kellie looked into the stores and houses lining the road, a couple of which were still in the final stages of being re-built. The town had come a long way in the last thirteen months and people were just beginning to get their lives back to some kind of normality. It was a fresh start for them all, which also felt good. The houses squeezed in between the stores were turning on lights and drawing curtains, as semi-darkness fell. Glancing in to see happy families once again going about their daily lives, a feeling of goodwill came over Kellie and she pedalled a little faster, now keen to get back to her own comfortable home. Reaching the end of Long Street, she swung around the corner towards her little house and almost collided with a tall stranger. There was no doubt in her mind he was not a local, so assuming he was a visitor, she hollered out an apology as she free-wheeled the last few yards. Although he was now behind her, the stranger automatically raised his hand in acknowledgment and stopped walking as he also called over to his dog, which had run onto the beach and was happily splashing about along the water's edge.

Running over to join in, the stranger laughed at his dog's antics as the animal continued to bounce through the shallow waters that lapped the edge of the shoreline. Picking up a stick, the man threw it along the beach, laughing as his dog hared off after it, then skidded on the soft sand as he drew up short to pick up the stick and race back to his owner, proud to have retrieved his driftwood trophy. Kellie had caught sight of this and turned to watch the two of them. She too was now smiling at the dog's exuberance and waved again to the stranger, who had seen her watching them. Feeling slightly envious of the fun being had in the last of the evening light, Kellie turned into her front garden and pushed the bike around the side of the house.

As she entered her home, thoughts of a warm bath sprang to mind and after putting on some relaxing music, Kellie filled the tub with warm bubbly water, before undressing and throwing her clothes onto the bed. Wrapping a warm and fluffy towel around her, she wandered across to the fridge to pour a glass of white wine, before returning to the bathroom. Having lit the two candles which sat on the end of the bath, she sank down into the bubbles. Thinking about Mrs Terry and holding her glass slightly aloft, she toasted the older lady and thanked her again for her ongoing friendship and kindness. It sure had been a strange day for them both and one that nobody would believe if she ever told them about it.

Kellie's evening and night passed easily and without the interruption of dreams about Ibrahim and ancient Egypt. Feeling some relief as she opened her eyes, Kellie was happy to see bright daylight shining through the curtains. Small birds were tweeting, which meant it must only be around six-thirty or possibly seven o'clock. But despite it being that early, Kellie was feeling wide awake. Throwing back the bed-covers, she bounced out of bed, cheerful and keen to start the day.

As was her regular morning habit, after brewing some coffee, Kellie took her first cup outside to sit on the veranda and enjoy the early morning sunshine. Settling down into one of the chairs, she was again impressed with the comfort of the replacement table and chairs that she had bought several months ago. They were much better than the ones taken by the twister, which she occasionally considered, as to where they had ended up.

With her hair still tied up and no make-up on, Kellie decided that she honestly didn't care what she looked like today, because she was feeling happier than she had in a long time, and that pleased her. Totally enjoying the comfort of sitting in her bright orange pyjama bottoms, which clashed perfectly with the purple strappy top she usually slept in, Kellie was no longer worried about who might see her looking so casual, which was a far cry from the townie version of herself that she'd left behind all that time ago. Kellie was comfortably relaxed, with her feet up on the opposite chair, enjoying her coffee as she watched the calm waters of the bay lapping the shore. It was going to be a perfect day and she felt totally at peace with the world and herself.

Whilst sitting quietly contemplating the previous day's events, a large brown dog bounced into view, closely followed by the stranger from the evening before, and as he glanced over to Kellie's house the man called out to her.

"Hi there, good morning! How are you today?"

Pleasantly surprised at his casual friendliness, Kellie responded with equal enthusiasm, "I'm fine thank you, and yourself?"

"Oh, well I'm just dandy thanks. Skip here is keeping me busy." He laughed.

Kellie noticed how bright his smile was against the tanned skin of his face as she called back, "So I see. He seems to love the water!"

Laughing, the guy responded as he walked towards her, "He sure does, since we arrived he's been in every day."

Reaching the front edge of her garden, he introduced himself, "I'm Steve by the way, Steve Michaels."

"Hi, Steve, I'm Kellie, nice to meet you." Kellie wasn't sure what to make of this encounter, but she was relaxed and happy and just smiled back. Completely unthinking about how she looked, Kellie was taken aback slightly as Steve spoke again.

"Nice PJs by the way," grinning at her now slightly embarrassed face, Steve just continued as if this was a normal conversation between them: "It's lovely to be able to sit and drink coffee, looking out at this stunning view first thing in the morning isn't it." Steve gestured with his hand towards the view across the bay, as Kellie forgot her embarrassment and smiled again, agreeing with him as she said how lucky she was. Steve clearly wanted to continue their conversation, which was easy and weird all at the same time; he was a total stranger, yet she felt completely comfortable talking to him, as he continued to ask her questions.

"Are you here on holiday?"

"No, I live here. How about you?" Kellie felt sure he must be a visitor because she had never seen him before and knew that she would definitely have remembered him; all 6'4" of that muscular frame, topped off by his sun-bleached blond hair.

Steve responded warmly, "Actually, I've just moved down from the city. My folks used to come here when I was a kid and I've always loved it, so when the opportunity came to escape, I jumped at the chance."

Kellie felt strangely drawn to this man and could hardly believe it when she heard herself offering him coffee and inviting him to join her.

"Sure, that'd be great, I'm pretty certain that Skip will be happy enough playing in the water." As Steve stepped onto her veranda, Kellie was amazed by how blue his eyes were, in fact they were so striking she was a little taken by surprise and hesitated for just slightly too long, as she accepted his handshake and offered him a seat. Bringing out the coffee-pot and another cup, Kellie sat back down and asked when and where he'd moved to.

Steve was happy to share his story, "I came down last week, but have been busy ever since then just sorting out the old place. It's one of the houses just along the beach. Do you know the one with the green tiled roof? It was desperately in need of some TLC, so I've been busy fixing it up."

"Oh yes, I know the one, that house has been empty for quite a while now. It's good to know someone has finally moved in to look after it."

Kellie was relaxed and happy. Steve seemed like a nice guy and was as comfortable in her presence as she was in his. As they sat and chatted, Steve told her how he had recently sold his construction business for a good price and decided to live an easier life by the beach. So, feeling inspired, he'd upped sticks and moved down to Rosada Beachtown with Skip. Whom he advised, was mightily pleased and despite his advancing years, was bouncing around like a young pup again.

It also turned out that Steve's folks used to rent a summer house a bit further round the bay, which is probably why the two of them had never met before, or at least why they didn't recall ever meeting. That said, both agreed that their paths must have crossed at some point over the years, because Steve also knew old Jack.

Time had passed quickly whilst they'd been chatting and as Kellie offered Steve more coffee, he thanked her, but declined, having just looked at his watch, before realising how long he'd been sat there. Apologising for taking up so much of her time, Steve politely excused himself and then asked Kellie that if she was free later, would she like to have dinner with him and see what he'd done to the old place?

"Actually, I don't really have any plans today, so yes, thanks, Steve, that would be lovely. I'll come along for around seven o'clock, if that suits you?"

"Seven o'clock sounds perfect, Kellie. I'll rustle up something which will hopefully be passable enough to qualify as a nice meal and then I can take the opportunity to show off my handyman skills." For some unexplained reason, Steve found himself wanting Kellie to really like what he'd done to the place.

The two of them laughed and on saying goodbye, both added that they were looking forward to dinner later. As Steve called Skip over, the two of them set off back along the beach towards their own new home.

After they'd gone, Kellie thought that she really ought to get dressed and catch up on some paperwork. Since owning the store, most of her free time had been absorbed by looking after the paperwork and partaking in her recently acquired skill of quilting, which she was surprised to find, she was actually rather good at. In truth, being so absorbed in the store had suited Kellie fine, because after Tom had died, she had needed something to immerse herself into and having to do everything by herself, had partially filled that void in her life. Besides which, it had been the only way she could cope with her grief.

Thinking of Tom, Kellie was overcome with a sudden feeling of immense sadness. As she sat staring at the paperwork in front of her, a tear escaped and ran down her cheek, splashing onto the papers. At that very same moment, Kellie sensed a sudden feeling of warmth and love completely surrounding her, just like when she and Mrs Terry had been in the store together yesterday. The sensation was so comforting that Kellie felt totally safe and very much loved. It was as if she could hear Tom's voice saying to her... *It's OK, Kellie. You're going to be fine, my love. The store looks great. You're doing a really good job and that Steve chap seems like an OK guy to me.*

Kellie looked across the room to the photo of Tom, which had been on display ever since she had sorted out his wrecked flat, following the twister. The picture was one of the two of them from when old Jack was still alive; they were sat on the edge of his boat and laughing at something or other. Kellie couldn't remember what it was they were laughing at, but she did remember the summer it was taken, because it had been her tenth birthday that year. Kellie recalled that fact from the outfit she was wearing in the photo; remembering the bright pink T-shirt and lime green shorts, which had been bought by her parents from the beach shop in town and which she'd spent almost the whole summer wearing. Both she and Tom had enjoyed a brilliant holiday that year and had spent much of their time together, with Jack and Lilly.

It was two years after that summer, when Tom's parents had been tragically killed in a car accident and he had moved into Lilly's home full-time. Tom spent the rest of his childhood attending the local school and learning many other skills from his beloved great-aunt, who so totally adored him.

"Oh, Tom, I do miss you." Kellie leant over to pick up the photo and planted a kiss on it. Holding his face close to her chest for a few moments, she sighed, then replacing it, she turned back to finish the paperwork.

As the afternoon wore on, Kellie decided to go for a walk to clear her head and after locking up the house, she started off in the direction of Steve's place. It was almost 6pm and the evening was beginning to close in as she wandered along the beach. Just before she reached Steve's house, Kellie spotted Skip tearing along the sand towards her, having escaped from the front garden. Stopping as he reached her, Skip accepted a much appreciated patting session and ruffling of his ears and as she took his face in her hands, she heard Steve calling for him. Looking up, Kellie could see Steve standing on the top step of his veranda. Realising that it was Kellie who was crouching over Skip, Steve stopped calling for him and instead, waved his arm, beckoning for her to come over. As she wandered across the sand, with Skip now circling her legs, Kellie laughed at his antics; he really was a lovable dog and just what she needed to push away her earlier sadness.

As Kellie approached Steve's place, she lifted her hand to wave back and calling out hello, went on to explain how she'd needed to clear her head after an afternoon of paperwork and decided to go for a walk along the beach before joining him for dinner. Luckily it seemed, just in time to catch the escapee.

Steve laughed and thanked her, he knew Skip would likely come back, but seeing as it was such a new place for the little fella, he was a bit worried when he'd noticed his dog wasn't in the house.

Steve held up the brush in his hand and explained that he'd been painting in the kitchen, but was almost done, so seeing as Kellie was already here, would she like to stay and have a glass of wine, while he finished off and then freshened up?

Kellie accepted Steve's invitation, saying *why not*, after all, Sunday was supposed to be a day of rest. To which Steve laughed and agreed, stating that he'd also been looking forward to having a relaxing evening, once he'd cooked dinner of course.

Kellie smiled back at him and accepting his offer, she followed him inside the house, immediately impressed by how tidy it was, most especially considering it had only been a week since Steve had moved in. By the looks of it though, he had already unpacked everything and seemed really well organised, which impressed Kellie. Telling him so, had Steve admitting he was actually a bit of a tidy freak. Whilst also acknowledging that yes, it *was* an unusual quality in a guy, particularly one with a Skip running around the place!

"Very true," Kellie laughed easily in response to Steve's humour. "You're really lucky to be so close to the beach though. I imagine with Skip spending so much time outside, he probably just collapses whenever he comes back in."

Steve nodded as he agreed, "Actually you're dead right, Kellie. Thinking about it, Skip does just crash out when he gets back from his run along the beach. I reckon it's all the swimming he does. He's not used to the freedom of being able to jump in the sea every day because back home, he was always out and about with me. Although, that was mostly just being at home, at work, or in the park, which only had a fountain, so there was no swimming for him there!"

Once again Steve and Kellie found themselves laughing and chatting together easily, whilst Steve finished the door-frame he'd been painting. Offering to show Kellie around, Steve wanted to impress her. Whilst for Kellie, having never been inside this house before, it was fun for her to explore it with him and hear about his ideas and plans on how he would fix up the place. Steve had already made a good start and there was not actually that much more to do, so it was easy for Kellie to visualise his thoughts and ideas on improvements. Steve also had a good sense of how the house could better be used by changing the use of some of the rooms. Kellie supposed his clever design ideas were due to his construction background and she liked that his thinking was completely different from how most people would automatically arrange the house. Yes, Kellie liked that about Steve, he was different, interesting *and* really easy to talk to.

Dinner turned out to be fresh fish, cooked to perfection with just the right amount of seasoning and served with buttered, crushed baby potatoes and a selection of freshly steamed vegetables. It smelt delicious and when they sat down at the table on the veranda, Kellie complimented Steve on how good the food looked. As she picked up her glass and raised it to him, the two of them smiled and at the same time said, *Bon appetite!* Laughing at the coincidence of saying the exact same thing, they took a sip of wine before setting their glasses back down and tucking into the meal. Which, Kellie was pleased to find, was every bit as delicious as it looked and having enjoyed the meal so much, she admitted to Steve that he'd surprised her with his culinary skills. Accepting the back-handed compliment, Steve confessed that he'd had a good teacher in his mother, who was a brilliant cook and had taught him whilst he was growing up. Not only that, cooking was so very different to his construction work and because he enjoyed it so much, he wasn't too proud to admit that it gave him a sense of release that nothing else could. Once again, Kellie was impressed, she really liked this guy.

The two of them enjoyed each other's company and chatted for hours, only realising the lateness of the evening when a cool breeze picked up. Thanking Steve for such a wonderful time, Kellie said she'd best make her way back home and thanked him again for the offer to walk back with her, assuring him it was perfectly safe and that she would be fine.

"OK, if you're sure then." But Steve felt uncomfortable agreeing to leave Kellie to walk home alone, so he was relieved when Skip jumped up and he grabbed at the opportunity of his dog needing a walk. Skip was actually fine and just jumped up because Kellie was leaving, which Steve knew really, but the fact was, he wanted an excuse to walk her home.

"Well it looks like Skip needs to go outside too, so why not let us walk with you? That way I'll feel happy to know you are home safe and Skip here will get to know the way back home from your place too." It was a flaky reason and he knew it, but Steve was also a gentleman and because of the lateness of the evening, he wanted to escort Kellie home. Grinning when Kellie relented, he patted Skip with a silent *well-done, boy,* as the three of them stepped off the veranda, to walk along the beach road footpath.

Secretly charmed by the fact that Steve had wanted to walk her home, as they reached the house, Kellie patted Skip goodbye and thanked her host again for such a wonderful evening, reminding him to drop into the store the next time he was in town.

"I'll definitely do that, Kellie. It'll be good to see what you've done with the place. Well, goodnight then and thanks again for a great evening."

As Steve walked away from Kellie's little house, he felt a warm glow inside and was really happy that he'd taken Skip for a walk in Kellie's direction that morning. Also, that his boy had run just far enough, for Steve to be able to stop and talk to the beautiful woman he'd almost collided with the previous evening.

Patting Skip's head again and now out of earshot of

Kellie's house, Steve voiced his thoughts out loud: "Thanks, Skip old boy, you're a little star. I think we've both made a new friend there. Kellie's great isn't she..." to which Skip just woofed and ran off again, pleased to have made his master so happy.

Chapter 8

Mrs Terry

The following morning was a little overcast when Kellie first woke up and there was a definite chill in the air as she opened the doors to enjoy her usual morning coffee on the veranda. Grabbing a wrap to throw around her shoulders and slipping her feet into some warm slippers, Kellie sat down to watch the morning tide return. Looking up at the sky she wondered if they would see the sun today. The summer had been kind to them this year, but it was fast drawing to a close and the chillier weather would be with them soon.

The drop in temperature of those few degrees definitely made a difference to the acclimatised locals, although for the many visitors that came most of the year round, it still felt relatively warm. Rosada Beachtown was in the far south where the climate was pretty mild all year round. Generally, there was no need for heavy winter clothes, with just a warm jacket or sweater being sufficient for the evenings. Kellie hoped they still had some warm weather to come before the cooler season started.

Steve and Skip woke up earlier than Kellie and had already been out for their early morning run, both having as much fun as each other, as Steve threw sticks of driftwood for Skip to chase after. Back at the house and feeling sufficiently exercised, whilst Steve prepared his food, Skip bounced around the kitchen, still full of excitement as he waited for his master to feed him. Laughing at his dog's happy demeanour, Steve put both bowls on the floor and leaving Skip to enjoy his food, he sat down to read the morning paper and enjoy his own breakfast – a favourite – which was scrambled eggs on toast, often followed by a slice of toast topped with the sweetness of honey, which was one of his guilty pleasures. As he finished his leisurely breakfast, Steve noticed that Skip was already fast asleep and legs akimbo, using every inch of the large cushioned bed that Steve had temporarily moved into the living space. Happily, that meant Steve could now finish off painting the kitchen, without Skip leaning against the wet paintwork, or trying to shove an enquiring nose into the paint pot.

Listening to the radio for company, it wasn't long before Steve was joining in and singing along to the old tunes from his teenage years. As he also reflected on the previous evening, Steve thought about how much he had enjoyed Kellie's company. He definitely wanted to see her again and the sooner the better. After dismissing all kinds of excuses, Steve finally settled on the idea, that he'd take a wander up town a bit later and casually drop-in to see Kellie, on the pretence of taking up her offer of a coffee and checking out her new store. Yes, he thought, that was a fine idea and one which, subconsciously, made Steve paint just a little bit faster and with a happy smile beaming across his face.

As Kellie busied herself around the store that day, she realised she was humming and feeling unusually happy, even more so since the sun had come out again. The store had been busy during the morning, but had now quietened down after the lunchtime period, which also gave Kellie some free time to work on her latest baby quilt. This one was for a little boy named Michael, who had only arrived in the world two weeks ago and was just adorable. As she worked away at her sewing machine, Kellie's mind drifted to the previous evening and thoughts of Steve. He seemed like a very genuine guy and had been a total gentleman towards her. It was like they had known each other for years already. Not only that, but he had cooked them a delicious meal and was actually quite funny. Kellie had very much appreciated his good company and it surprised her slightly, when she realised just how much she truly had enjoyed their evening together. In fact, since Tom had died, that had been the first evening she had actually spent alone with anyone, other than her parents.

Tom's smiling face came into her mind and she sighed wistfully. Having shut herself away both physically and emotionally after losing Tom, Kellie had put all of her energy, time and effort into re-designing and running the store. But, now that she had broken the ice which had frozen over her social life, Kellie realised how much she had missed chatting to another person over dinner and last night, she recognised she had so enjoyed doing just that, spending time with Steve.

Previously, whilst Kellie had lived in the city, there had been guys that she had dated, but there was nobody who had really managed to light her fire and with her change of lifestyle, since moving to Rosada Beachtown, there had been no burning desire to go out and meet new guys. Kellie had been quite satisfied with the friendship that she and Tom had shared and as they always spent so much time together, there had really been no need, or even space, for anyone else to come into her life.

Nobody else had even come close to being on her radar in the past, but Steve had definitely captured her attention last night. That much was certain.

Thinking about it now, Kellie realised that it had been quite a while since she had even dated a guy. As in normal, everyday dating. The reality of the whole dating scene had not been familiar to Kellie for a very long time, yet she had not even missed the hyped-up environment she'd often found herself in, when dating in the city. Out here in Rosada Beachtown, people seemed more genuine and definitely they were a lot more relaxed and far less worried about impressing someone. They were real, which to her meant they were truly open, honest, very down to earth and totally genuine people. In Rosada Beachtown, there were no flashy bars or nightclubs, just a few relaxed and friendly restaurants, with a couple of café bars along the beach that the locals and visitors shared and enjoyed. It was odd really, because having never thought about it that way before, as she was mulling it over in her mind, Kellie knew without any doubt that her future was set in Rosada Beachtown and she absolutely loved the comfort that certainty gave her. In fact, Kellie couldn't imagine ever living anywhere else now.

In the back-room of her store, as the hands on the clock displayed ten minutes past three, the old-style bell sounded, letting Kellie know someone had entered. Luckily, she was almost at a suitable place to stop working on the quilt and so in her usual friendly way, called out to her unknown customer.

"Hello, I'll be right with you. I'm just finishing something off."

Leaving her sewing behind, Kellie continued speaking as she entered the front of the store, looking up at the person waiting to see her, made her stop in her tracks. Steve was browsing while he waited, having left Skip back at the house snoozing peacefully. As he looked at her, Kellie beamed and blushed simultaneously, causing Steve to grin back at her.

"Oh, hello again, Steve, what a lovely surprise. I didn't expect to see you again so soon…" Kellie's voice trailed off slightly.

"Ah yes, well, I was just in town and so I thought I'd pop in to thank you again for a lovely evening." It was Steve's turn to blush, he felt slightly awkward, but only because he really liked Kellie. Right at this moment though, he felt like he was twenty-one again, wanting to ask a girl out on a first date, but not knowing quite what to say.

Kellie smiled at Steve, feeling really happy to see him again, as she replied, "It is I who should be thanking you for that delicious meal, Steve. I really did enjoy it. The whole evening I mean." Kellie was clearly feeling slightly flustered and so Steve saved her blushes by glancing around the store and commenting on it.

If she only knew the truth, which was that he too was feeling a little flustered by her closeness to him and that gorgeous smile, seemed to draw him in and leave him powerless.

"The store looks amazing, Kellie. No wonder you are so busy here, there is so much to see. You have some really unusual stuff in here too. It's not your everyday store that's for sure." Steve was impressed and it showed on his face. Kellie accepted the compliment graciously and thanked him, because even though it seemed unnecessary, she also felt slightly relieved that Steve liked her store so much.

Not wanting him to leave quite yet, she offered him a drink, "Do you have time to stay for that coffee?"

It was what he had hoped Kellie would ask him and Steve bravely admitted as much to her as they both then laughed at his little ploy. The awkwardness now broken, allowed the previous evening's easy-going mood to return. Kellie was quite happy to allow Steve to follow her through to the back-room and invited him to have a look at the quilt she was making, whilst she re-filled the coffee maker. Glancing round, his eyes filled with interest as he noted and soaked everything in. Then he spotted the goblet, still stood in its usual place at the far end of the work-bench, just within reach of Kellie's touch, as she thought of and remembered Tom every day. Following his gaze, a brief look of sadness crossed Kellie's face and on seeing that look, Steve felt concerned and dared to ask her about it, as he reached towards the goblet, but then recoiled without touching it.

"This is unusual, Kellie, you don't see many of these around. Where did it come from?"

"Ah yes, the goblet," Kellie sighed gently as she turned to pick it up and lovingly stroke the precious stones set within it. "There is a long and very sad story attached to this."

"Well, if you're happy to share the story, I'd be interested in hearing it and besides, I'm in no rush to get home." Steve was intrigued and wanted to know what had caused that sad flicker to cross her beautiful face. Kellie put the goblet back down and handed Steve his coffee, as she began telling him the story of how the goblet had come to be in hers and Tom's possession. As the two of them walked back into the store, they sat down in the very same place where Kellie had sat with Mrs Terry. Kellie dared to share with Steve how the goblet had come to mean so much to both her and Tom, including the funny feeling they had each experienced whenever they touched it. Also, how she still touched it every day, usually whenever she entered and left the store, just to say hello and goodnight to Tom.

Unsure of how Steve would react, Kellie decided not to share the longer story of Ibrahim, Jocelyn and Simona and how they were all linked to the goblet. That would need to wait for another day, once she knew Steve a little better.

"I guess that sounds a bit crazy to you?"

"Actually, Kellie, I think it's a lovely thing to do," Steve smiled at her. "It proves how close you and Tom were. Such friendship is precious and I'm just sorry that I never got to actually meet him, he sounds like a really decent guy. It's a tragedy what happened to him. He was very brave to protect you like that."

Kellie was touched by Steve's reaction and response as she spoke of Tom. She had of course already shared her story with Steve during the previous evening, explaining how she had come to own the store, her childhood friendship with Tom and how he had died. Also, how she had in fact loved him more than she had ever told him, or even realised herself, until it was too late. Steve seemed to be so understanding of her feelings, his kindness and compassion surprised her once again. Tom would have liked Steve, Kellie felt sure of that and she told Steve so.

"It sounds like we could have been really good mates, Kellie." Steve wanted to change the subject because Kellie now looked very sad and he wanted to see her smile again. To distract her, he told her what he'd been doing that day, including how Skip had just crashed out again when they'd got back from their run.

After admitting that his attempts at singing along to the old songs on the radio were best left for his ears alone, relief flooded his thoughts as he saw Kellie's sadness lifting and she laughed at the imagined scene. Then of course, there was his visit to town, in the hope that she would be free for coffee, to be followed by his plan to call in and see his Aunt Biddie. Well actually, Steve explained, Biddie had been a family nickname, her real name was Charlotte and she wasn't really a blood relation, but an old friend of the family who he'd grown up knowing as Aunt Biddie.

Hearing Steve refer to Aunt Biddie as Charlotte, made Kellie pause midway through drinking the last of her coffee. Returning the cup to its saucer, she gulped and leant forward slightly as she almost whispered her question: "Do you mean Mrs Charlotte Terry?"

Kellie blanched as she waited for the nod that came from Steve as he replied: "Yes, that's her, Charlotte Terry. Why? Do you know her?" Steve sounded surprised and then he realised that of course, with Rosada Beachtown being so small, Kellie probably knew a large majority of its population.

"Yes, I do know her, she's been an old friend of mine

and Tom's for as long as I can remember; in fact, she and Tom's Great-Aunt Lilly were best friends." Kellie's hand shook slightly and she clattered her cup as she placed it on the table. Looking up at Steve and remembering her conversation with Mrs Terry late Saturday afternoon, Kellie suddenly felt worried and slightly sick. Why hadn't she gone to check on her this morning? Kellie couldn't answer that. Yet, she remembered feeling as though Mrs Terry had been saying more than her usual goodbye the last time she had seen her. But it was also as if Kellie was meant to leave her to go home alone, to be freed from this lifetime and the burden of guilt that Simona had carried during the many hundreds of years since that awful day when she had killed Ibrahim. Standing up from her seat, Kellie looked worried and told Steve she had a really strange feeling about his Aunt Biddie, then stating that she was going to close up the store early and would come with him to see Charlotte Terry. Understandably, Steve was slightly thrown by Kellie's reaction, but he was also delighted that Kellie would be happy to go with him to see his aunt.

How the heck was Kellie going to explain to Steve about the dreams and his aunt's admission, or even Kellie's own suspicions that Mrs Terry's soul may already have passed into the spirit world? How could he possibly understand all of that? Plucking up courage, from a source she didn't realise she had within her, Kellie began to tell Steve part of the story.

"Steve, you know I said Mrs Terry, your Aunt Biddie, was an old friend? Well, she is and I've always looked upon her as kind of extended family. However, she came to see me Saturday afternoon, which ordinarily is quite normal, but this time it was to discuss something very personal to us both and when she was leaving, well, it felt like she was saying more than her usual goodbye." Kellie reiterated her fears, "I have a very strange feeling, Steve.

I'm not sure your Aunt Biddie is going to be..."

Kellie was about to say the actual word, when Steve interrupted her, nodding as he explained that since he'd arrived in the store and seen the goblet, he'd been feeling odd in himself, but had put it down to his imagination and because of the story of the goblet coming from ancient Egypt. But the truth of the matter was that Steve also knew there was an Egyptian connection with his Aunt Biddie, although he had decided not to mention it to Kellie at that moment, because he didn't want to upset her even more than she had appeared to be. It was obvious to Steve that Kellie was clearly very concerned about his aunt and because of her concerns, he decided they'd best get to Charlotte Terry's house quickly.

Rushing up the street, the two of them fell into a worried silence and barely spoke, other than to say they both hoped she was OK. Charlotte Terry's house was very old, with a huge front door and rooms with high ceilings. Lifting the heavy door knocker, they waited to give the older lady time to get to the door and welcome them in. But there was no reply and no warm welcome. Steve remembered he still had Aunt Biddie's spare key. Having visited her the day after he arrived in Rosada Beachtown, and whilst the water had been disconnected at his beach house, his dear aunt had loaned him her spare key and very kindly offered the use of her shower and washing machine whenever he needed it. Now, turning the key in the lock, he pushed open the large door and entered the house with Kellie by his side.

Steve called out, "Hi, Aunt Biddie, it's me, Steve, are you home? I have Kellie with me. Hello, Aunt Biddie, are you home?"

There was no reply and the house was in semi-darkness from where the curtains had not been opened that day. With a sinking feeling in the pit of her stomach, Kellie knew and Steve suspected the worst as they walked upstairs. Hoping they were wrong and still calling out, they knocked on the main bedroom door. An eerie silence settled and only the grandfather clock ticking away down in the entrance hall of this grand old house, offered any response.

Steve turned the handle and reluctantly, the two of them entered Charlotte Terry's bedroom; they were right, she was there, still and quiet. Steve's dear Aunt Biddie, Kellie's darling Mrs Terry, was lying in her bed. Whilst her small frame looked tiny under the bed-covers, her face was completely relaxed and looked just as though she were still sleeping. The scene was peaceful and perfectly serene. Silence filled the room. Steve stepped forward to touch his aunt's forehead with the back of his fingers, knowing that he would feel her skin already cold to the touch. Steve looked up at Kellie and then back to Aunt Biddie, tears filled their eyes as they both accepted that she had passed. Kellie gently brushed her old friend's hand and whispered *goodbye*, as she then touched Steve's arm and said they should call the Police Chief.

Steve was shocked, he had only seen Biddie the day before yesterday and she had seemed fine to him. Telling as much to Kellie, he supposed that it was just that she was old and it was her time. Kellie nodded, remarking at how peaceful Mrs Terry looked and that she must have just gone in her sleep. The two of them agreed there was no better way for her to have gone and expressed how it must have been a pain-free passing, because she looked youthful and beautiful again. It was as if she were at one with her very soul and just resting in the calmness of that room.

Steve and Kellie went back downstairs and from the telephone in the entrance hall they called the Police Chief, who asked them to please wait and not to touch or move anything in the house until he arrived. The two of them stepped outside and waited for the Police Chief's car to pull up in front of the house.

Kellie was glad that Steve was there, he knew so much more about Mrs Terry's life and who her remaining family were, so he would be able to help with telling the right people. The Police Chief also called the coroner, who arrived shortly afterwards and confirmed that although it was not a suspicious death, he would of course need to perform an autopsy to confirm the cause. The coroner then took away Mrs Terry's body. Thanking the young couple, the Police Chief asked Steve if he would like to inform the family himself, to which he replied that yes, he would take care of things. He added that he would also ask the family to contact the coroner's office, as well as the Police Chief himself, as soon as they were able.

As Steve and Kellie were left alone in Mrs Terry's house, the two of them hugged each other; both of them felt sad for Mrs Terry and each needed comforting for their own sense of loss of their lovely aunt and dearest friend. Steve said he would call his parents first and then call Aunt Biddies' sister, Madeline; whom he expected would relay the news to the rest of Biddie's family. Adding that no doubt the family would then need to come down and sort out the house.

Kellie understood only too well what that would involve.

As Steve walked over to the telephone, Kellie said she would go and find them both a stiff drink, feeling sure that Mrs Terry wouldn't mind if they had a small brandy each, knowing how they had both suffered such a big shock.

As Steve picked up the phone and dialled his parents, Kellie walked through to the living room and pulled back the curtains to let what was left of the daylight into the room. As she did so, she glanced around the room and gasped, for the furnishings and ornaments had a decidedly Egyptian feel about them. The fabrics were rich and luxurious, with so many different textures and colours covering the cushions, chairs and couches. The heavy curtains were made from silken blue and gold brocade and suited the style of the room perfectly. But what caught Kellie's eye the most was stood on the mantelpiece, resting on a purpose made mount and looking as if it represented a reminder of a distant past and what that past had held. It was actually a quite beautiful, if not a little sinister, golden dagger. The handle was very ornate and decorated with coloured stones, the blade was long and slightly curved at the end, easily long enough to be tucked into a belt, or hidden in the folds of a long garment. But it was the colour of the gold that reminded Kellie of hers and Tom's goblet. She shuddered as she looked at the dagger, afraid to move close enough to touch the beguiling ancient weapon.

Kellie was staring at the dagger from across the room as she moved to pour two glasses of brandy; feeling wary of the dagger's power, she almost spilled the golden liquid over the side of one glass as her hands shook involuntarily. She could hardly believe it, surely not, after all the years and centuries that had passed, surely this couldn't be the dagger that Simona had used to kill Ibrahim?

But it was.

Both the dagger and goblet had come into the possession of the same archaeologist, who had discovered them in a tomb he was helping to excavate on his last trip to Egypt. During the return journey and with a significant number of treasures already stashed in his own luggage, the archaeologist had subsequently passed on the dagger to the parents of Charlotte Terry. Who, as it would turn out, was the baby daughter of the Captain in charge of the paddle steamer that had brought the archaeologist and his wife back from their voyage of discovery, many years ago.

Carrying the glasses of brandy out into the entrance hall, Kellie handed one to Steve, who was still talking to his parents. They were understandably shocked and upset at hearing the news and said they would travel down if he needed them. Steve thanked them for the offer, but said he was fine, that he had met Kellie, who was a friend of Aunt Biddie's and that he would call them again in a few days.

The next phone call was going to be the hardest, so Steve took a swig of the brandy and as Kellie sat beside him on the stairs, he called Charlotte Terry's sister to break the sad news. It was such a shock that Madeline asked if she could call him back the following day. But not yet having a telephone line connected, Steve had to give her the number for Kellie's store instead. It was the only other telephone number they had between them, so Kellie offered to be a point of contact for the family. It was the least she could do for Mrs Terry. Kellie had also taken note of the coroner and Police Chief's direct numbers and offered them to Steve to relay to Madeline.

By the time the calls were finished and the house locked up again, the sky was turning dark. The sun had long since sunk towards the horizon, with barely a smidgen of it showing, encouraging the darkness of night-time to close in. Steve offered Kellie his arm as the two of them made their way back into town and down to the beach. Both feeling drained and in need of company, they strolled along to collect Skip, before walking down onto the beach and letting him run along the sandy shore, as they headed back towards Kellie's place.

Sitting on the veranda and looking out at the rippling inky black water, they watched Skip happily playing in the semi-darkness, oblivious to the sadness of the evening. The two new friends each remained quiet as they sipped their steaming mugs of hot chocolate that Kellie had prepared. Both of them needed the comforting drink, having decided the brandy they'd drunk earlier was probably best left at just that one. Neither of them had an appetite for food, although Skip did pester them for a snack, which had Kellie raiding the fridge for something meaty to give to him. Cold sausages did the trick and Kellie was happy to give them to Skip, who wolfed them down in no time and ran off to play in the water again. Skip's antics soon had both Steve and Kellie chuckling, which was just what they needed to break their sombre mood.

Chapter 9

The Future

In the following days, Charlotte Terry's family arrived to clear out her house and to settle the arrangements for her funeral. After a little deliberation, prior to their visit, the family had decided that the memorial service and funeral would take place back home with them. Madeline, who preferred to be called Maddy, was immensely grateful to both Steve and Kellie, and very much appreciated everything that they had done for her beloved sister, Biddie. She thanked them warmly, having accepted their generous offer to assist her with sorting out Charlotte Terry's house.

Steve helped during the daytimes, but Kellie could only help out after her store was closed each day. It was a monumental task deciding which belongings would be kept, which would be sold or given away and sadly, which would just end up in the trash.

Despite the family's new found 'oil wealth' Maddy was very much in touch with her roots and had always longed for Biddie to move closer to their own family home. But nothing could drag her elder sister away from the sea and the big old house she had loved so much. It pained Maddy that only now, in death, would she have her sister close by, when they finally lay her to rest in the family plot at their local cemetery.

Trawling through Charlotte Terry's house, as they uncovered several delightful and beautiful belongings, Kellie and Steve grew ever more aware that they were looking into the deeply personal life of their dear Mrs Terry, Aunt Biddie. Although both of them felt increasingly uncomfortable, for Kellie, it stirred up memories of sorting out Tom's flat and so several times, she had to take a deep breath and step outside to gather herself again.

As they reached a suitable point in the proceedings, Steve suggested they now leave Maddy to sort out the last of his Aunt Biddie's things. Having offered to sell some of the unwanted items in Kellie's store, the two new friends wished Maddy well and took their leave, but not before asking her if it would be acceptable for them both to attend the funeral and memorial service.

"Why of course, my dears. Biddie would absolutely want her family and friends to be there and so would we. It will be upstate of course, in about ten days' time, but I will write the address down for you and drop it into the store before I leave town."

The older lady smiled at them both and took their hands before continuing.

"Thank you both so much, you've been such a great help. I'm sure my husband Alec and I would probably still have been here next week without your help, you've been fantastic and I'm so glad that Biddie had you both around her during her final days."

After hugging Maddy and saying their goodbyes, Steve and Kellie set off together to walk down to the beach and their respective homes. Steve thought Skip would need a run and as the two of them needed to eat, he suggested they wander along the beach to the café bar. Kellie agreed, feeling happy to have Steve's company and knowing Skip would be more than happy to bounce around in the water as they walked along beside him.

Wanting to talk about something other than his beloved Aunt Biddie and the clearing of her precious belongings, Steve remarked to Kellie how he still couldn't quite believe how Skip seemed to be going through such an energetic second puppy-hood since they arrived. Right on cue, the excitable dog charged up and down the sand towards them, then in and out of the water to shake off the wetness, which of course sprayed all over them, causing Kellie to screech with laughter as the cold water showered them both.

"Do you know something, Kellie. I reckon that moving to the beach is going to be the best thing me and Skip ever did."

Smiling at Skip, Kellie replied, "He does seem to be enjoying a new lease of life here, Steve, that's for sure."

Steve knew that *he* was too; he hadn't felt this relaxed and contented in a very long time. Not only that, Skip was happy and they were with Kellie. As he spoke, he wondered what more either of them could possibly need.

"Yes, he does, doesn't he. And you know something, Kellie, I do too, and I am so very glad that I almost bumped right into you the other night."

"Me too, although I'm glad we avoided an actual collision, that could have been very messy." Kellie laughed at the memory. "It is funny how things can turn out, don't you think? Sometimes it feels like certain things are just meant to be. It's like everything is just perfectly right in that very moment."

Steve also totally got that same sense of everything just being right.

"I know exactly what you mean, Kellie, and I'd like to thank whoever it is up there, looking out for us both right now. They're doing a great job!"

Steve surprised Kellie with that comment, yet at the same time, she felt a tingling inside her that she couldn't explain.

Reaching the café-bar and aware of Skip being wet, they chose to sit outside and enjoy the fresh air. With him safely tucked under the table, they shared some delicious tapas style dishes, enjoying the many different flavours, accompanied by several glasses of Sangria, which the owner poured for them.

As they finished their meal, Steve suggested they go

114

for a longer walk with Skip. It was a lovely evening, the air felt surprisingly warm and balmy and the temperature was just perfect for a stroll along the sands. As they walked, Steve started talking about his Aunt Biddie and some of her amazing possessions that they had been fortunate enough to see. He also remarked on how uncanny it was that there was an Egyptian link between Kellie and Aunt Biddie.

That connection had not been lost on Kellie and she agreed that it was really uncanny, whilst also remembering their last conversation and the very real reason for that link.

The two friends chatted comfortably as they walked and Kellie occasionally bent down to pick up a small stone, admiring its smooth surface as she rubbed it between her fingers, before then throwing it back into the sea and laughing at Skip as he chased into the water after each one.

Steve picked up a piece of driftwood which he also threw for Skip, who decided to then swim along with the oversized piece of weathered wood in his mouth, whilst maintaining a parallel line to his master and Kellie, as they strolled along the beach. After a while the group of three turned around and as they started walking back, Steve began to tell Kellie the story that Aunt Biddie had told him so many times over the years, in fact, ever since he'd been a small boy, during the many summers he'd spent in Rosada Beachtown.

It began with two Egyptian lovers, who were forbidden to be together and how there had been another woman, who was also madly in love with the same man. This other woman had secretly loved the man ever since she had first laid eyes on him, but she had been unable to express that love, because he was already in love himself, with the woman he was employed to protect. Aunt Biddie had told the young Steve, how the dagger which stood on her mantelpiece had belonged to that other woman. Also, how she had tragically used it to kill the very man that she loved, when she realised he was never going to be hers. It was a story which had been told to Aunt Biddie by her father, who in turn had heard it from the archaeologist that had given him the dagger so many years ago. Aunt Biddie had also told the young Steve never to touch the dagger and that when she eventually died, the dagger was to be buried with her and must *never*, under any circumstances, be passed on to anyone. Steve had made sure that he told Maddy about the dagger and his dear Aunt Biddie's wishes. But of course, Maddy already knew, she had grown up knowing about the dagger and as her dear sister wished, she assured Steve, it would be laid to rest with her.

Kellie could hardly believe what Steve was telling her; it was the same story, which explained a little of why she had felt so certain of the connection between the two of them, her and Steve. She also knew that Mrs Terry was part of that connection and Kellie now felt as if the old lady were encouraging her to tell Steve about her dreams and what Charlotte Terry had told Kellie the night before she died. Kellie took a deep breath and began her story. It was Steve's turn to be astounded as he listened intently to what Kellie was telling him, it was his Aunt Biddie's story, but with all the details behind the history of the dagger!

"Wow, so you mean *you* were that woman, *the Lady Jocelyn* and Aunt Biddie, *my Aunt Biddie*, was the other woman, this Simona, the woman who killed Ibrahim?"

Steve was beyond speechless, he couldn't believe what he was hearing; one, because the connection between the two women was so uncanny and two, because his Aunt Biddie was such a gentle soul, who he knew would never have hurt anyone in this lifetime. Kellie understood his confusion and reminded Steve that

Simona was from Mrs Terry's past life and that she, as Simona, had utterly regretted her actions and even pleaded forgiveness. Which of course Kellie, as the Lady Jocelyn, had been unable to give, back then, but because she was able to provide that forgiveness during this lifetime, Kellie now believed that Charlotte Terry's spirit was finally able to rest.

It was barely conceivable how these two women were connected in both lifetimes and that Simona's soul had lain dormant inside of Aunt Biddie until the right moment had presented itself for her to speak out. Steve felt stunned by the story.

"So, for all of her years in this lifetime, Simona's soul had stayed with Aunt Biddie, until she could meet her love-rival, the Lady Jocelyn? You, Kellie, and at an appropriate time when, as an adult in this life, she could again ask for forgiveness?"

"Yes, Steve, I truly believe that is how it turned out."

It was almost too tragic really and not only that, as Kellie reminded Steve, Tom had also been part of the story, being the protector of Kellie in this life. In truth, he was Kimea, Ibrahim's personally trained gladiator, a trusted protector who was to succeed him, in looking after Jocelyn during her ancient Egyptian life. Kimea had fulfilled that role once again in this life. Kellie herself found it hard to believe, but she was finally convinced and said as much to Steve, as the two of them stopped walking and turned to face each other.

"So you see, sometimes, things really are meant to be, Steve."

"It sure is an incredible story, Kellie, the parts we both know, but what about now and having met me? How do you feel that I fit into this story, today, in our lifetime?"

Kellie's eyes misted as she looked into the deep pools of blue that searched her face for answers.

"You, Steve, I don't know if you came from that past

117

life. Maybe you did. But whether you did or not, I truly believe you are here to nurture and nourish my soul for this lifetime. I think we were meant to meet and I think...'

At that point, Steve breathed a sigh of relief and smiled broadly as he interrupted Kellie; taking her hands in his, he lifted them to his lips and kissed them gently as his eyes admired her, drinking in the loveliness of her face and that beautiful smile.

"You know, that's such a big relief, Kellie, to hear you say those words. Since I first saw you, I've been unable to forget you and I feel strangely drawn to you. It's funny, it's like you are right and that we were meant to meet. I feel like we truly are meant to be together and right now that feels so strong that I need to, I want to, that is, if you're OK with it? What I mean to say is, may I kiss you, Kellie?"

Kellie smiled happily back at Steve and squeezed his hand as she nodded and stepped closer to him; he could smell her perfume as he breathed in the warm air that surrounded them and gently pulled her towards him. Their hearts were pounding as the dying sun glistened on their skin and their warm lips met.

And so it was, that just as the sun began to set and fill the sky with golds, pinks and purples, the two-soon-to-be-lovers kissed, their hearts soaring as they did so, both knowing that as their lips touched, they belonged together.

Part 3

Chapter 10

Saying Goodbye

Charlotte Terry's funeral was mainly a family affair, but even so, Kellie and Steve were warmly welcomed by the whole family, all of whom were comforted by the fact that these two young friends had cared for Maddy's dear departed sister as if she had been their very own family. It had especially warmed Maddy's heart to know they had shared Biddie's life over the many years she had spent in Rosada Beachtown. Today though, was one of their saddest days as each said their goodbyes to the wonderful sister, aunt and dearest friend, known to so many of them simply as 'Biddie'.

Having brought her sister's body back home from the town she had spent most of her life in, Maddy had wanted to follow all of Biddie's final wishes and so, as promised, she had placed the golden dagger in her casket. However, because the family had changed their choice of funeral from a burial to a cremation, Maddy had been advised by the curator that it was best to remove the golden dagger from the casket – his reasoning being that it would just melt down and be gone forever, with the gold then belonging to the state, rather than being able to stay with her deceased sister. This change of plan had Maddy worried, not just about the dagger not staying with Biddie, but also because she didn't want the gold to simply be taken by the state. Reluctantly, Maddy acted on the curator's advice and removed the dagger.

Now having to come up with an alternate plan, which she hoped would still please her deceased sister, Maddy thought of passing the dagger on to Kellie and Steve. Yes, she thought, she could do that tomorrow because Kellie and Steve were staying overnight. Maddy imagined they would recognise that whilst she and Biddie would no longer own the dagger, its history would be understood and protected by both Kellie and Steve.

The following day, as Kellie and Steve said their goodbyes to the family, Maddy thanked the two of them for all they had done for her darling sister and for making the journey up-state to come to her funeral.

"But before you go, I have something for you both and please don't be mad with me." As she explained the curator's recommendation to her regarding the dagger, Maddy added that she was also hoping they would accept it both as a memento of her darling Biddie, *and* as a thank you for the love and friendship they had each shared with Biddie over the years.

Kellie and Steve were more than a little surprised at this revelation and news, but they waited patiently, as Maddy went to fetch the velvet-lined box containing the golden dagger. Kellie began to feel a sense of trepidation.

Returning, Maddy opened the velvet-lined box and took out the golden dagger which had sat on Charlotte Terry's mantelpiece for so many years. Kellie stepped back. Not only did she never expect to see the dagger again, she was reminded of its sinister connection as Maddy placed the golden blade into her open hands, pleading with her to accept it as a token of friendship and love.

The coolness of the stones which were set into the handle of the ancient weapon pressed into Kellie's palms; but as she politely accepted the surprisingly heavy blade from Maddy, a cold shiver ran down Kellie's spine.

Receiving this artefact was not expected and Kellie felt really uncomfortable holding it, whilst also not knowing quite what to do with it. As her pulse started racing, Kellie could feel her heart beating faster. As she turned to Steve, feeling slightly panicked, Kellie witnessed the same uncomfortable look on his face too. Steve was remembering how his Aunt Biddie had always said the dagger must be buried with her and under no circumstances should it be passed on to anyone; he couldn't believe that the dagger was still here and not melted in the crematorium furnace.

Maddy's smiled faded a little at seeing the almost worried expressions on their faces and now feeling a little nervous, she quickly passed Steve the now empty box, suggesting he should perhaps take the blade from Kellie and replace it in the velvet lining. Then, trying to dismiss their obvious concern, Maddy hugged them both and wished them a safe journey home to Rosada Beachtown. Reminding them that as her sister's house was being sold, it was unlikely they would meet again, Maddy wished them both a happy future together and remarked once again, how lucky Biddie had been to have them in her life.

It all seemed to have happened so quickly and unexpectedly, that as the two of them drove out of the ranch-style property, Steve and Kellie fell into a shocked silence, each absorbed by thoughts of what to do with the golden dagger, which was now lying inside its box on the back seat of their car.

Kellie spoke first, "What do you think we should do with it, Steve?"

Knowing exactly what she meant, but not how best to answer her, Steve paused before he replied: "I really don't know, Kellie, but what I do know is, the dagger was supposed to be buried with Aunt Biddie and she wouldn't be happy knowing it was still around and with us now." Steve held a vision of how he thought his aunt would have reacted, had she witnessed the hurried handing over of the ancient Egyptian dagger.

As Kellie spoke again, a sinking feeling was growing in the pit of her stomach: "I think I should lock it in the safe when we get back, until we decide what to do with it. We can't pass it on, that would be wrong, and if we bury it, someone could dig it up again." Pausing, she then added, "Oh, Steve, I really don't like it being left with us."

Steve agreed, "I don't like it either, Kellie, but I think that's a really good idea. Let's keep it in your safe until we can decide what to do with it."

The word 'we' was deliberate. Steve recognised that his feelings for Kellie were developing fast and he hoped they would share a deeper, lasting and very meaningful relationship. From the moment they had kissed on the beach, during that awesome sunset, Steve had been smitten and more than anything, he wanted Kellie to be his, to love, to protect and to cherish forever. That wasn't too much to ask, was it? Steve's thoughts were straying away from the dagger, so he smiled reassuringly at Kellie, before returning his eyes to the road, ever cautious of the fact that he wanted her to feel safe with his driving.

Trying to lighten the mood, Steve asked the question he had been pondering on for the past few days: "I wonder what Aunt Biddie would say about us knowing each other, Kellie."

Kellie laughed and said she had no doubt that Mrs Terry would approve because of what she recently said to Kellie about always smiling – y*ou never know who is falling in love with your smile* – and Kellie did smile as she relayed Mrs Terry's advice to Steve.

"Indeed, that is true."

Steve's quick response made Kellie blush at realising what she had just said. With a cheeky grin, he continued, "Yes, she sure was a wise old bird was Aunt Biddie."

Despite knowing her full name, Kellie had always referred to the older lady as Mrs Terry, which had been a throw-back to her childhood and one of the respectful titles that all grown-ups expected to be known by. It was something taught in most schools back then and was widely adopted across the population of their state. Kellie felt sure the familiarity of first names for grown-ups would come eventually, as generations evolved, but for her, and dear old Mrs Terry, time had stood still in that regard.

The journey home was taking a good while and after the emotional events from the previous day, it wasn't long before Kellie began to feel sleepy. Steve suggested she tilt the seat back slightly and have a little doze, reassuring her that yes, he was fine and not at all tired. In reality, he was a little tired of course, but Steve didn't want Kellie to fret and besides, he quite liked the idea of her sleeping beside him as he drove them both home.

But while Kellie slept, Steve's thoughts were given free reign as he remembered the last time he had seen his aunt and the events between that day and today. He would miss Aunt Biddie and silently wished that she could have lived just a little longer, to know that he had met her friend Kellie and how she had affected his life so positively. As he dwelled on that thought, Steve also hoped his Aunt Biddie would have approved of his choice of wife, for he felt certain that he would one day marry the now sleeping Kellie.

As Steve glanced down at Kellie's sleeping face, he was struck by her clear skin. The sun was shining through the side window and kissing her golden locks as it highlighted her beautiful long eye-lashes that seemed to reflect the brilliant sunlight. The roads were quiet with very little traffic and as Steve's mind drifted, he sub-consciously eased his foot off the accelerator. Luckily, and only because theirs was the only car on that particular stretch of road, Steve was thankful he hadn't caused any bother to other drivers as his car slowed down. Feeling concerned at his momentary lapse in driving concentration, he pulled over to the side of the road for a moment and drank in Kellie's beauty, as he silently acknowledged that he really was falling for her in a big way.

125

As he watched her, Kellie stirred and asked if they were home already. Steve felt embarrassed and hurriedly said that he just needed a quick stretch of his legs. Jumping out of the car very quickly, he walked around the back of it, feeling relieved that Kellie hadn't caught him watching her and pulled a few stretches before getting back into the driving seat. Thankfully, Kellie had drifted off again, which surprised Steve, but then remembering her involuntary penchant for weird dreams, he guessed she was also one of those lucky people who could sleep anywhere. As they started off again, Steve switched on the radio, keeping it low so as to avoid disturbing Kellie whilst he listened to the latest tunes emanating from the car speakers. Only another hour to go and they would be home. Steve was really looking forward to seeing Skip again. He'd never left his dog overnight before and he was very grateful that Jim and Martha Collins were able to help them out. It was really kind of them and he was sure Skip would have been no trouble at all.

When the final mile passed under the wheels, Steve was grateful to see the 'Welcome to Rosada Beachtown' sign, and as if by some psychic vibe, Kellie stirred, also noticing that they were almost home.

"Gosh, I'm sorry about that, Steve, I must have needed the sleep." It was Kellie's turn to feel embarrassed.

"It's no problem at all, sleepy-head." Steve grinned and added: "I thought we could pick Skip up before we head home. If that's OK with you?"

"Sure, of course that's fine. I'm sure he'll be so excited to see you, I bet he's missed you like crazy." Kellie was looking forward to seeing Skip herself and thought how they could all do with a nice walk along the beach, or run, in Skip's case!

Pulling up outside Jim and Martha's, Kellie glanced across the street to her store, which had been closed whilst they'd been up-state. The sign in the window explained Kellie was away for a family funeral and that normal opening hours would resume tomorrow. Just in time for the weekend trade, thought Kellie. As she worried about the potential business she had turned away whilst the store wasn't open, Steve remarked on how good the window display looked and complimented Kellie on her window-dressing skills, to which Kellie preened, feeling pleased that Steve was taking such an interest in her business. It was so precious to her and she loved it when anyone complimented her store.

Walking up to the entrance of Jim and Martha's own store, they could hear Skip barking excitedly from the back yard; he had heard Steve's car and could now also hear their voices. Martha welcomed the two of them home and graciously accepted their appreciation and thanks for looking after Skip. Jim said he'd loved having Skip staying with them, adding that it had reminded him of when little Oscar had still been around. As the four of them chatted, Skip came bounding into the front of the store and almost jumped into Steve's arms, as dog and master shared their excitement at seeing each other again.

Smiling as they watched this happy event, Kellie suggested that Jim and Martha should come over for dinner with them on Sunday, so they could thank them properly, to which both Jim and Martha gladly accepted, saying they'd look forward to it.

"Excellent, we'll see you Sunday then!" Steve approved, as he, Kellie and Skip, took their leave. All of them laughing as Skip raced over to the car.

Dropping Kellie's bag off at *Jack's Place* first, they then drove along to Steve's house and parked the car. After unloading, they went for a long walk up the beach, throwing small sticks of driftwood for Skip and laughing as he bounced in and out of the water chasing after them. It surprised the two of them how much they had missed the beach over the past couple of days, but now back in familiar surroundings, they relaxed and Steve caught Kellie's hand, as they strolled along the sand, shoes in hand, chatting about Biddie and the past few days.

The two of them were happy, apart from the looming issue of what they were supposed to do about the golden dagger. Both were still undecided and found it easier to postpone making any firm decisions.

Chapter 11

Jack's Place

Life was improving with every day that Kellie and Steve shared and as they grew closer and closer, the love developing between them was one that neither had experienced before. Yet for them both, it felt so utterly natural and they very much enjoyed just being together. There was no need for any pretence, what they had was very real. Kellie's parents had also met Steve and warmed to him immediately. Both feeling relieved and happy to see their daughter had finally met someone who made her smile again. Also hoping he would be the one with whom Kellie could look forward to a bright future with, one full of hopes and dreams.

Paul and Barbara believed that Tom would most definitely have approved of Steve, which brought a welcome comfort to them both, as they spent more and more time getting to know the man their daughter was so obviously in love with.

Several months passed by without further incident and Kellie's store continued to thrive. Steve had finished the work on his own house and was very happy with the end result, particularly the new downstairs, which was now quite open plan, but designed in a way that complimented the traditional colonial style of the house. The veranda had some new low level comfy seating, as well as a small table for dining and offered a relaxing space to enjoy the beautiful coastline views that stretched their way around the bay. It was the perfect place for spending balmy evenings together, relaxing, whilst Skip was playing on the beach in front of them. Their lives were just about as perfect as they could be; peaceful, calm, and for Kellie, very healing.

Steve had taken to popping into the store occasionally to help Kellie, in between fixing up his house. But now that it was finished, he was chomping at the bit to do more for her. However, due to the fabulous renovation the insurance company had achieved, there was nothing he could really do to improve the store, or even Tom's old flat above it. Both were in tip-top condition and whilst that was ideal for Kellie, it also meant that Steve now needed to find something else to keep him busy.

Since moving to Rosada Beachtown and having met and fallen in love with Kellie, Steve had no desire to move away, but he needed something useful to do, which would also keep him busy and fulfilled. Because even though he didn't really need the money, Steve also didn't want to sit around and become a spare part, in his journey of life on earth. So, thinking about the key skills he already possessed and knowing that home renovations were something he really enjoyed doing, the obvious choice seemed to be something along those lines. Kellie agreed, having already realised how important it was for Steve to feel useful, particularly when it came to his newly adopted community.

From those joint discussions and thought processes, Steve started doing small jobs for the towns-folk, which he found to his great delight, was also a great way to meet new people and expand his friendships in the town.

The two of them were really happy and as the weeks passed by, Kellie and Steve began to talk of moving in together. It seemed like the most natural next step for them and having 'spoken' to Tom about it, Kellie felt he would be OK with that decision. Of course, it was actually Tom's photo that she had spoken to, but as she also felt his presence around her, Kellie was sure he must be listening to her. As she smiled at Tom's photo, Kellie had explained that she was in love with Steve and they were going to move in together. But that didn't mean that she had forgotten Tom, far from it, she loved him and always would. Tom would always be her oldest and dearest friend, which is why it just felt right telling Tom that she was happy again and that even though she missed him every day, life had to go on.

The fact was that Tom had watched over Kellie from the spirit world and he could see how excited and happy she was. He was grateful that Steve was there although his own heart-strings strained at wishing it could have been him, for he too had loved Kellie, just as Kimea had also loved the Lady Jocelyn in ancient Egypt, after Ibrahim had died.

Because Steve's house was the larger of the two that they owned and because they also had Skip to consider, it made perfect sense for Kellie to move into Steve's house. But this new change was a bittersweet moment in her life and Kellie felt guilty at leaving behind another part of her life. It was hard enough no longer having Tom at the store, but to also be leaving *Jack's Place*... the thought of moving out of the little home that had seen so much change in her life, saddened her a little.

Steve understood and tried his best to reassure Kellie by reminding her that whilst she was *moving on* with her life, that was different to *leaving it behind* and besides which, both Jack and Tom would want her to carry on living and to be happy doing so.

Kellie knew Steve was right and whilst she had always appreciated how incredibly lucky she was to have been left both a home and a business, she would have given it all back in a heart-beat if she could have old Jack and her darling Tom back in her life. Losing them as well as Aunt Lilly and dear Mrs Terry, had been a hard cross to bear and was still quite incredible to her, that she had already lost four people so precious to her heart.

This timing just means it's the perfect moment to move on, my dear – the voice of Mrs Terry sounded in her head, causing Kellie to nod and agree as she spoke out loud, "Yes. Yes, you're right, Mrs Terry. It most definitely is time to move forward with my new life."

Yet, despite all of that, there was still a slight twinge of sadness within her.

Kellie decided to rent out *Jack's Place* as a summer-let, which seemed the right thing to do with it, because there was no way she would ever sell the home that still meant so much to her. Besides which, letting out the beachside house would help to bring in more income, meaning she truly would be comfortable financially, so if the store fell on hard times, she would not have to worry so much. Yes, life really had turned around for Kellie, albeit through a great deal of personal tragedy and pain.

As Kellie and Steve packed up her things and began moving them into Steve's truck, he suggested they also re-name the green roofed house, so that it felt more like *their home* rather than *Steve's place.* Kellie loved Steve for his thoughtfulness and told him so, grinning at him, as they began trying to think of different names. Steve suggested that whoever chose the best name, would buy the other one dinner, which made the whole experience great fun and was just what Kellie needed to distract her from the sad thoughts of leaving *Jack's Place*.

Steve was keen for Kellie to feel like his home was now her home too and so he truly hoped she would be the one buying dinner, because that meant she had also chosen the new name!

It was hot work packing-up and cleaning the house, so as they moved the last boxes into the truck, Kellie and Steve decided to sit on the veranda for a bit to cool down and share a glass of bubbles, as they said thank you to *Jack's Place* for taking good care of Kellie. In the late afternoon sunshine and before the sky turned to pinks and oranges, as the sun inevitably sank towards the horizon, Steve also reminisced about how he had shared his first coffee with Kellie on that veranda and how Skip had been his resourceful excuse to wander down to her part of the beach. The two of them laughed at the happy memories and clinked glasses to toast Skip, as well as old Jack, thanking him for his wonderful beach-house.

Their discussion about house names had by now, been running for a couple of hours, but as they sat there in the sunshine, Kellie said, "You know, Steve, I'd really like to name the house something completely different from all the others along the beach road."

Steve looked thoughtful, waiting for Kellie to continue: "OK, go for it... what do you have in mind?"

Kellie now had no other name in her head except one and it seemed so right that she hoped Steve would love it to. "Well, what do you think of *The House of Galilee?* Does that appeal?" Kellie was surprised at the biblical name herself, but it had just popped into her head and didn't seem to want to leave.

"Hmmm, *The House of Galilee*, that has an oddly familiar ring to it, but you know what, Kellie, I actually do love it!" Steve was genuinely excited about the name Kellie had chosen and he raised his glass saying, "Let's drink to our *House of Galilee!*" Steve grinned as clinking Kellie's glass he added, "Oh and that also means dinner is on you!"

Kellie laughed too and agreed. Steve leant towards her and taking her free hand in his, he raised it to his lips, brushing a gentle kiss across her fingers, as if sealing their new life together. She was home, truly home; Steve was her future, her happiness, her love, her hopes and her dreams, all rolled together to complete her life.

The universe was smiling down on the young couple and Ibrahim himself was delighted that Kellie had found him again in Steve. Their lives together truly were eternal.

Kellie was feeling a little giddy, both with happiness, the glass of champagne and the effect of Steve's obvious

133

love for her; she was deliriously happy and couldn't wait to share *The House of Galilee* with Steve. So as the last drop of bubbles were consumed, the two of them got up and after a final check of *Jack's Place*, they locked the doors and jumped into Steve's truck, to drive the very short distance along the beach road to their new home.

On hearing the truck pull up outside, Skip was up and out of his bed, standing behind the front door and wagging his tail like mad, eager to welcome home his master and new mistress. Kellie laughed when they walked through the door as Skip jumped up against Steve, the two of them bonding with a good ruffling of fur, before Skip switched allegiance to welcome more pats and cuddles from Kellie. The house was finally a home and they really were their own little family.

Steve said he would bring the boxes in from the truck so that Kellie could carry the lighter ones into the relevant rooms, ready to be unpacked. It was a welcome and easy arrangement and the two of them worked well together, comfortable in each other's presence. Luckily, there was plenty of room for Kellie's belongings, Steve had made sure of that because he wanted Kellie to feel that there was enough space for her in *their* home and not as if she, or indeed her belongings, were too much and just being squeezed in.

After shifting the heavier boxes for Kellie, Steve said he'd just take Skip for a run along the beach, leaving Kellie to unpack essential items for that evening. They had both decided to leave the bulk of the unpacking until the following day, so that tonight, they could just share a meal and relax for the rest of the evening out on the veranda. The champagne had worked its magic on them both and they were now feeling more romantic than practical.

As the last of the sunset sank towards the horizon, the sky changed again from the stunning display of pinks and hot orange, to the dusky grey light that precludes the darkness of the night sky. Despite the greyness of the light, the evening was a remarkably balmy one for the time of year and just perfect for sitting outside to enjoy the simple pasta dish they'd thrown together. The two of them could not be happier as they shared their meal and finished the bottle of bubbles. It was after all, an evening of celebration, which included Skip also receiving an evening treat.

Later that evening, after clearing away the dishes and with the day's excitement still burning in their bellies, Steve turned to Kellie and taking her in his arms, he kissed her passionately. Skip was already settled into his bed as Steve took Kellie upstairs to theirs, pausing at the bedroom door to lift her into his arms. Carrying her gently, he placed Kellie on the bed and stood up as he began undressing. Their growing passion was intensified as Steve, in all his naked glory, knelt onto the bed and began undressing Kellie; the button through dress she had changed into earlier, was easy for him to undo and Steve gasped as, pushing aside the opening of her dress, he fully revealed her pert breasts. She was naked and wanting, ready for him to take her and as Steve touched Kellie's skin, his own hardness began to grow, much more than he had expected. So turned on was he by his beautiful Kellie, bending forwards, he kissed her lips, her face and her neck, before running his soft lips across her breasts. Taking her hard nipple into his mouth, as he sucked on it gently, he heard Kellie let out a sharp gasp of pleasure. Steve's fingers simultaneously reached down to explore her femininity, causing Kellie to arch her back again and again, as her desire burned for this man, whom she realised that she loved beyond anything, or anyone else in her life before this day. Reaching to touch his hardness, Kellie pleasured Steve until he could stand it no more and as he entered her welcoming warmth, the two of them

135

joined into one rhythmic, pulsating, passionate burst of hardness and acceptance, as the seed of Steve's love made its way into the soft, receiving belly of the woman he loved and wanted to marry.

As their passion subsided, Steve and Kellie lay panting and satisfied, their intense love-making leaving them unaware of its result, which was now settling into the comfortable lining of Kellie's womb. Caressing this woman, that he loved so much, Steve was convinced he wanted to be with Kellie forever and he whispered the words without any doubt in his mind.

"Marry me, Kellie. I love you so much and I want to spend my life with you. Will you marry me?"

Kellie was surprised by Steve's unexpected proposal, but she too felt like they were meant to be together and so she replied equally without doubt and with a beaming smile on her face.

"Yes, Steve, I will marry you. I love you more than I can tell you..." and before she could finish her sentence, Steve crushed her lips with a kiss so passionate, that they again shared their bodies as his hardness grew with every inch of passion and love that he felt, until it burst once again, this time causing Kellie to cry out as her own orgasm exploded, joining his, "Oh my God, Kellie, what have you done to me? I'm yours my darling, totally and utterly yours, forever." Steve's voice was thick with the passion and love that was overwhelming his heart and soul. And as he held her in his arms for the longest time, the two of them slept, cuddled together, their love having been consummated in the fullest sense.

Chapter 12

Breakfast in Bed

The following morning, as the sun rose and the birds began tweeting, Steve stirred first. Kellie had warned him that she liked her sleep and so he slipped out of bed to go downstairs and make them coffee with toasted cinnamon muffins. Half an hour later, adding fresh juice to the tray, Steve made his way upstairs as Skip watched his master from his own bed. It was still early and Skip wasn't yet ready for his morning run.

Placing the tray on the bedside table, Steve stripped off his shorts and slipped back between the sheets, awakening Kellie as his strong arms gently pulled her towards him. He kissed her forehead. Kellie was warm and snuggly as she cosied up to Steve, happiness exuding from every pore of her being. Smelling the coffee, she thanked Steve for bringing them breakfast and as her sleepiness left her mind, Kellie reached for him again, wanting to enjoy every moment of their first morning together as the soon-to-be Mr and Mrs Steve Michaels. Steve responded in what can only be described as a suitably satisfying manner, honouring the woman he was happy to say would soon become his beautiful wife. Their morning passion was as evident and all-consuming as the night before. Whilst the coffee grew cool, along with their breakfast, they didn't care, they were in love and were going to be married and nothing and no one could be happier right at that very moment.

Steve loved Kellie – every inch of her – inside and out and Kellie loved Steve; for his strength, his passion and his undeniable love and protective care for her very being. What more could any woman want?

As they finally left their bed, breakfast having been

consumed in spite of the coolness of it, Steve said he'd better take Skip out. Kellie was in a playful mood and with it being Sunday, she didn't have to work, so she suggested they go for a swim to clean their love-making from their bodies. It would be invigorating she promised, as she laughed at Steve's concern over cold sea-water, versus a hot shower. But like Kellie, he too was feeling carefree and so he embraced the thought of the morning sea, daring them both to swim naked and feeling mildly surprised when Kellie took up the challenge.

As the two lovers entered the water, they were suitably attired, after all, it was a public beach, but once under the water, their costumes were off and the two of them swam and embraced, swimwear clutched tightly in their hands. Steve's hardness turned Kellie on so much, that it was as though the two of them had untapped resources of passionate energy as he lifted her out of the water, briefly exposing her breasts and hard nipples. Steve's excitement grew and he pulled her under the water again to privately caress those hard nipples, whilst he kissed her passionately. Their passion was intense and with the water supporting their now tired legs, Steve lifted Kellie up and gently slid her down onto him. Kellie gasped so loudly, she was sure the people in the nearby houses must have heard her, but she didn't care, all she knew was that she was in love with Steve, as he thrust up into her again and again, the two of them concealed under the water, with only the fish to witness their conjoined bodies once again being satiated by exploding orgasms.

As they struggled back into their costumes under the water, the two of them were grinning at each other over their moment of naughtiness; they were having so much fun, that neither could be serious, especially as their now jelly-like legs felt even heavier as they walked out of the sea. Totally wasted and with no energy left, the two of them fell onto their towels, whilst Skip bounced around them, spraying them with sand and causing them to ruffle his fur before throwing a stick for him to fetch. Thankfully, Skip had been happy chasing gulls and splashing about in the shallows whilst Steve and Kellie had been absorbed by their own frolicking, so he had not witnessed the conjoining of his master and mistress, but he was happy to see them together and that was all he needed. The three of them stayed on the beach until they were dry. When they eventually walked back towards their *House of Galilee*, both Kellie and Steve were in need of a shower to wash away the salt and sand. Steve said he was definitely in need of more food and coffee, to give them a boost before unpacking the remaining boxes containing Kellie's belongings. Kellie giggled again and agreed she too was ravenous after their morning exercise.

By the end of the afternoon, they had unpacked everything, marvelling at how much quicker it was to unpack, than it had been to pack it all at *Jack's Place*. Kellie was very happy with the space Steve had cleared for her and she felt immediately welcome and comfortable with living in *their* house. The kitchen cupboards would need some adjustments, what with them both now cooking in it and with Kellie's extra kitchen bits. But they had both agreed they would probably need to shift things about a bit, as they got used to living and using the space together. It was quite remarkable how well they and Skip were blending as a family though, which was something both Kellie and Steve were very aware of and grateful for.

As time progressed, they began living their everyday lives, interspersed with long beach walks and dining on the veranda, as well as working in the store and of course, Steve's handyman business, which was already popular with the locals. Life together was very settled as they began to plan their wedding. Both of them wanted a simple affair and decided that the beach outside *Jack's Place* would provide the perfect venue, with drinks and a rum-punch, along with a buffet style table of food and, as a special treat, plenty of dancing to one of the local steel bands, *Nevada Ho*, which was named after the next township around the coastline. As a town, Nevada Ho had a large Caribbean population and music was a big thing in their town, with several steel bands travelling around the local areas, performing for all kinds of occasions. Kellie loved the sound of a steel band and Steve thought it was a great idea to have one, especially as they would be spilling out onto the beach. Steel bands and beaches were a great combination and the perfect choice for their wedding.

The plans were made and friends got roped in to help on the food front. It really was going to be a simple, traditional, community-style occasion, with bunting strung across the house and front garden, tables and chairs borrowed from friends and neighbours, most of whom would be joining them for their beachside party. It all sounded so perfect for them, that neither Kellie nor Steve could think of a better way to celebrate them becoming man and wife.

Word soon spread among their community, with Jim and Martha being the first to congratulate them and offering help wherever it was needed. Everyone wanted to make this day of celebration one they would all remember and thrive on for years to come. Kellie and Steve's wedding was exactly the kind of boost that their little community needed, after the horrors of the day the twister came to town.

Feeling very aware of how beloved Tom had been to everyone that knew them both, Kellie needn't have worried because everyone had welcomed Steve. Having known that Kellie and Tom had been such good friends, most of them believed that Tom would absolutely approve of Kellie's choice of husband. Steve Michaels was well regarded in their community and had become very popular with many of its residents, as his good nature and reputation for skilled workmanship was shared and appreciated by everyone who engaged him. Martha and Jim were almost as thrilled as Steve and Kellie themselves, such was the happiness at hearing this news and an infectious excitement quickly spread throughout their immediate community.

The big day was to be four months later, when the weather was more reliable and to give everyone plenty of time to make all the necessary arrangements. Several stores even decided to close up for the afternoon of the big day, thinking that many of their customers would likely be at the party anyway. So, it began, the countdown to their big day!

Paul and Barbara were a little stunned on hearing Kellie and Steve's excited news, knowing that the two of them had only known each other for just under a year. But, they were also ecstatic for them both, remembering when they themselves had first met and despite what others had said at the time, how they just knew that they were going to spend the rest of their lives with each other. Steve's parents, Pam and Dave, were equally thrilled and insisted on helping out with paying for the wedding, offering to cover the drinks bill for them. Both Steve and Kellie were feeling incredibly lucky to have such wonderful parents and so many fabulous friends to share their very special day. Life was very good indeed.

Paul and Barbara had wanted to pick up the cost of Kellie's dress and offered them a lump sum of cash to put towards a honeymoon. Whilst thanking them for their generosity, Kellie told her mother that actually, she wanted to wear her Grandma's dress, which was from the late 1920s. Kellie just loved the style of it, and the fine lace looked handmade. Barbara was delighted and of course, cried a few tears. Happy tears she said, because she knew that her mother would have been over the moon to know that her grand-daughter would be wearing the 1920s dress.

The soon-to-be newly-weds couldn't believe their good fortune and after thanking both sets of parents, they stepped outside. Alone once again and looking up at the stars, with hands held together, the two of them thanked the universe for bringing them together and for the amazingly kind generosity of their parents.

Steve was happier than he had ever been, or thought could be possible. He could hardly believe that Kellie really was going to be his wife. Who could have possibly imagined that this would happen to him, when he and Skip had first moved to Rosada Beachtown and the green-tiled house on the beach road?

Steve's own parents were equally surprised at how his life was turning out and because they had loved Kellie from the moment they first met her, the news of the wedding was like the icing on the cake for them, as they secretly contemplated the patter of tiny grandchild feet. There was no doubt though that they were both excited and thrilled at the new future which lay ahead for their son and his beloved Kellie.

That night, Kellie's dreams returned, although a little more abstract than usual, with a mixture of what she had dreamt previously, about ancient Egypt, Jocelyn and Ibrahim... and now Steve, in the present day and the two of them on the beach on their wedding day.

When Kellie woke up from her dreams, she felt as though Ibrahim was giving her his blessing. *He must be happy for me*, thought Kellie, but as that thought crept into her waking mind, so did Tom. Kellie wanted to believe that Tom would be happy for her, but there was an uneasiness creeping over her and she wondered if maybe Tom would have different thoughts to those she imagined. Thinking it must be pre-wedding nerves, Kellie dismissed her wild concerns and got up out of bed to prevent her from dreaming again. Steve was still sleeping, which was unusual for him, but as Kellie's weight lifted from the bed, he stirred and opened his eyes just in time to see his naked wife-to-be walking across the room.

"Good morning, beautiful."

Steve smiled as Kellie looked towards him, her breasts were in silhouette as she turned to blow him a kiss and tell him she loved him. Reaching for her silky robe, she wrapped it around her body before pulling open the drapes and flooding their room with the early morning daylight. Kellie moved back towards the bed and kissed Steve, "I'll go and make us some coffee," she said as she coyly slipped from his eager hands and laughing, made her way downstairs to meet an excited Skip, who'd jumped up from his bed, to welcome his new mistress to the new day that had dawned.

Whilst the coffee brewed, Kellie walked out onto the veranda and watched Skip as he ran around the side of the house, safely hemmed in by the white picket fence which now formed the border of their property. The sea looked wonderfully blue and Kellie was relieved to see that the sky was also clear of clouds. It was going to be a nice day, one that will bring in the customers Kellie thought, before turning to go back inside and take their coffee upstairs. The two of them were both working that day and so they were soon showered, dressed and breakfasted.

Kellie kissed Steve goodbye and made her way to the store. Skip was lucky enough to be going to work with Steve, who was ever grateful when a customer loved dogs and insisted Steve bring Skip with him every day. This time it was so his customer's daughter could enjoy playing with Skip, whilst Steve fitted their new kitchen. That was a request Steve was very happy to agree to, he much preferred to be able to take Skip with him when he was working. Skip of course, felt exactly the same and loved all the extra fuss and attention bestowed on him.

Chapter 13

One Surprise After Another

Kellie and Steve's wedding plans had been finalised. Everything that could be done, had been taken care of, leaving their lives to continue normally for the next few weeks. All was well and both Kellie and Steve couldn't be happier, as one particular day, not long before their wedding, Kellie went through to the safe to look for a few individually boxed jewellery items, to replenish stock in the glass counter. Kellie was humming a tune she had heard on the radio that very morning, as she carefully pulled out all of the neatly stacked papers. Hidden behind the papers were various boxes containing several small, yet valuable treasures. As Kellie reached to the back to retrieve the last box, she realised that the only one left in the safe was the velvet-lined box containing the golden dagger.

After Mrs Terry's funeral and with no idea of what to do about the dagger, Kellie had kept it locked away, carefully obscured by everything stacked in front of it. But being so well hidden, she and Steve had almost forgotten about it whilst going about their daily business, although both knowing a decision was needed.

Kellie now pulled the box out nervously and carried it across to her work-bench. Sat on her work-stool and staring at the closed box, whilst contemplating its contents, she glanced across to the goblet, which was still sat in pride of place, as her daily reminder of Tom. An uneasy sensation was filling the room and as Kellie looked back at the boxed dagger, even though the store was empty of customers and she was alone, her senses were confusing her. To Kellie, it felt as if there were several people surrounding her, watching and waiting, all the

145

time wondering if she would open the box. She did. Now taking the golden dagger out of its velvety lining, Kellie held it up close to the goblet. The two ancient Egyptian artefacts truly were beautiful and very pleasing on the eye. It was only the dark secret of their past which marred their present beauty and was something that could never be changed.

As Kellie continued to stare at both the dagger and the goblet, she became aware of an invisible presence stood next to her, comforting her. The name Ibrahim came into her mind once again and she knew he was with her. She couldn't see him, but she could *feel* him. Intrigued by this sensation, yet not in the least afraid, Kellie asked a question out loud.

"Is that you, Ibrahim? Are you here with me?"

Of course, there was no obvious reply, but Kellie just knew that he was there with her and so she spoke to him again.

"Ibrahim, is there something you want to tell me?"

Nothing. No response. Just an overwhelming sensation surrounded her, filling her mind as it urged her to use the goblet on her wedding day.

"I will."

Kellie had spoken the words out loud, but then felt a little silly doing so, knowing there was nobody there, let alone anyone actually listening. The moment felt very surreal to her though and whilst she could not explain it, Kellie sensed that Ibrahim could hear her, so she asked him another question.

"What should I do about the dagger?"

A cold sensation ran down Kellie's spine again and she felt the need to put the dagger down on the work-bench. Suddenly feeling very heavy and cold, Kellie really didn't like holding it. Patiently, she waited for a response, but none came. Feeling frustrated and wanting someone to tell her what to do, Kellie returned the dagger to its box and bending down, quickly pushed it to the back of the safe. Still not knowing what she should do with it, but knowing she definitely did not want to keep it, Kellie returned the front of the store, to continue with her initial task of replenishing the glass display counter, whilst trying to ignore the dagger that now seemed to be drawing her thoughts back to ancient times.

That evening, relaying what had happened to Steve, Kellie asked him what he thought they should do with it. But like Kellie, Steve really didn't understand how this was all happening, or what to suggest, and so they again decided to just leave the ancient dagger locked away where it was, for the time being at least.

However, he did tell her that he had some really exciting news, which was that he had booked a surprise honeymoon destination for them! Steve seemed very pleased with himself at the choice he had made and he was clearly desperate to share the news with Kellie.

Knowing Kellie's long interest in ancient Egypt and because of the goblet and dagger connections, Steve had found a cruise along the Egyptian section of the River Nile. His enthusiasm was obvious as he explained how they would touch into various different Egyptian towns and places of interest, throughout their journey along the Nile, including Cleopatra's very own riverside residence! Almost beside himself with excitement, Steve was thinking that he must surely have chosen the most perfect honeymoon for Kellie.

Kellie herself was a little stunned at the serendipitous coincidence between her handling of the dagger on the very same day that Steve had booked an Egyptian honeymoon for them. Although feeling a little pensive, she knew she wanted to go, there was no doubt about that. She had always wanted to visit Egypt, right from when she was studying ancient Egyptian history in university. But, it was the events involving the goblet, losing Tom, Mrs Terry's admission at being the historical Simona, before she too was gone, and now the golden dagger too, that was creating turmoil in her head. All of that, along with her dreams, meant the overwhelming feeling inside her was of both intrigue and trepidation. But, the thought of walking within the ruins of Cleopatra's palace and knowing she had been there during her lifetime as the Lady Jocelyn, meant that Kellie not only wanted to go back, but she was destined to.

Not wanting to worry Steve or dampen his obvious excitement and enthusiasm at choosing Egypt for their honeymoon, Kellie refrained from telling him exactly how she was feeling and instead, joined in excitedly with his plans. As they talked into the small hours, it also became obvious to both Kellie and Steve, that they should take the dagger with them to Egypt. It was as though they were being instructed to do so, but without there being a person or voice doing the talking. Both Kellie and Steve felt sure there must be a place in Egypt, where they could leave the dagger behind and so rid themselves of the worry and coldness they experienced whenever they thought of it. Steve said they must find a way of transporting it safely, without the bulkiness of the box it was currently sitting in. Kellie agreed and suggested that they probably also needed to get special permission to carry the artefact across country borders. Neither of them wanted to find themselves in trouble with their own or the Egyptian authorities, should they be found transporting it.

"Good thinking, Kellie, the last thing we need is to be locked in an Egyptian prison on our honeymoon!" Kellie laughed, lightening the mood.

Steve left the arrangements for transporting the dagger with Kellie to organise. Joking aside, he recognised the importance of them taking suitable advice, which, as it turned out, was not as complex an arrangement as they expected. A call to the Foreign Office pointed them to a specific team, who then forwarded several forms to be completed and returned with requested photographs, to prove their ownership before they left their own country. It really was that simple and once all the paperwork was received, completed and returned, they felt able to relax and just look forward to their very special trip.

As their wedding day approached, Kellie and Steve grew evermore excited, because not only were they to be married, but Kellie had also realised that she was indeed carrying the seed of Steve's loins in her belly. The early morning bouts of sickness and the test with her doctor had confirmed the happy news. Kellie was pregnant! It was still early days, but having worked out dates, it became obvious to her that their baby *must* have been conceived the weekend Kellie moved into their *House of Galilee*. That realisation made the news even more precious and once she had told him, Steve agreed with Kellie that it was good karma for them both. Even though both of them were surprised at the unplanned news, they were also utterly delighted and agreed that it didn't matter to them whether the baby was a boy or a girl, as long as it was healthy.

Steve was overjoyed. He was going to be a father! Kellie laughed as he danced around their home, with Skip bouncing beside him and wondering what all the excitement was about. Kellie was still a little stunned at the news, but she too was extremely happy, ecstatic in fact and soon the three of them were all dancing around, until Kellie, feeling slightly dizzy, said she needed to sit down. At once, Steve turned into the protective husband and father-to-be, insisting she put her feet up while he fetched her some water. Kellie laughed, saying she would be fine, whilst quite enjoying the attention Steve was showering upon her. She could not be happier and as she rubbed her hand over her tummy, Kellie spoke to her unborn baby for the first time.

"Hello, little one. You know, you are the most precious little thing and we are going to love you so, so much. We cannot wait to see you."

Skip nestled his head into Kellie's lap, as if he now knew there was soon going to be a new person for him to love and protect. Kellie stroked Skip's head and smiled at him, telling him about their new addition to the family.

When Steve returned with some water, he suggested they should call their parents to share the fabulous news! Even though it was very early days, Kellie agreed. She was feeling as excited as Steve was and said to put the phone between them, so they could both hear their parents' reactions.

As they dialled the first number, although they didn't admit it to each other, both Kellie and Steve were slightly concerned that their parents would disapprove of how fast their lives were changing. But they needn't have worried, both mothers cried tears of joy and the soon-to-be grandpas were equally delighted, and proud, as they congratulated their off-spring and shared their combined happiness about not only the upcoming wedding, but also their unexpected grandchild. The good news just kept coming they said, which made the grins on Steve and Kellie's faces spread even wider.

With the wedding just days away, Kellie began to worry that her tummy might be too big for the dress. Sharing her fears with her mother, Barbara reassured her daughter that due to the style of the 1920's gown, it would be fine and that her tummy wouldn't even show. Kellie felt a little relieved. Although she was very proud at being pregnant, she didn't want her bump to be too obvious on the day of their wedding because they wanted to keep their exciting news within their families for just a bit longer.

The countdown calendar Steve had put up in their

kitchen highlighted the fact that their wedding day was just a week away and with so many people wanting to celebrate with them, it seemed like almost half of Rosada Beachtown would be on the beach that day. But Steve and Kellie didn't mind at all; they wanted a traditional community wedding, and that is what they were going to have.

In the days before the wedding, Martha popped across to Kellie's store several times to check all was well and to see if there were any arrangements which needed her assistance. Grateful for Martha's help and support, Kellie reassured her friend that all was in hand and that they were expecting both sets of parents to arrive that evening. Martha also reminded Kellie not to forget to take the goblet home with her, for a final clean before the wedding. Thanking her for the timely reminder, Kellie told Martha how happy she was that Steve had agreed they *should* use the golden goblet as the first cup they would drink from, after becoming husband and wife.

Unbeknown to Martha, Kellie also felt that Ibrahim would have approved and hoped that Tom would too. But Martha, who must have read her mind, said at that very moment, "You know, Kellie, I think Tom would have loved that you and Steve were using the goblet on such a special day. I only wish he were here to see you get married."

Martha sighed and as she glanced at Kellie, tears were beginning to well in her eyes, as she thought of her darling Tom. "I wish he was too, Martha." The two women hugged each other to help ease their sudden sadness.

Previously, when they had first announced their wedding to Jim and Martha's family, their daughter Maria had offered to look after Kellie's store whilst the newlyweds were away on their honeymoon. It had seemed like the perfect solution, especially when Martha supported her daughter's offer by saying she could also pop across throughout each day to check on Maria. Kellie had eagerly agreed. It was a good arrangement and she knew Maria was more than capable of running her little emporium, having grown up helping out in her own family's store. Both Kellie and Martha felt confident that Maria could cope. In fact, her kind offer had also lifted a huge weight off Kellie's mind; knowing Maria was so willing to help out had saved the worry of having to close-up the store for the two weeks they would be away.

For Maria, it would be good experience and she was thrilled, having long admired Kellie's new store, ever since it had re-opened. Also, having spent many hours in the store with Kellie, Maria was more than happy to help out and was keen to gain some independence and responsibility, which, running the store for two weeks, would absolutely provide. It was a chance for Maria to prove herself – both to herself and her parents – at how much she had grown-up. Although if the truth were known to her, both Martha and Jim were very well aware of how quickly their daughter had turned from a child, into a beautiful and capable young woman. It scared them a little, knowing she would likely flee the nest soon.

However, also unbeknown to them, Maria was not planning to flee the nest anytime soon and in fact, very much like Kellie she too wanted to stay in Rosada Beachtown. The truth of the matter was that Maria hoped this two-week period would also give her a chance to prove herself to Kellie, so that when Kellie and Steve's baby arrived, Maria could once again step into the breach and help them out, longer term.

Finally, the wedding day had arrived and Steve and Kellie were thrilled to be joining their lives together. Forever bound by love and name, as they took their vows, watched and applauded by their family and friends, which included many of the people from their local community.

The sun shone and clear blue skies and calm sea, provided a perfect backdrop for the whole day. The band played brilliantly and as Steve offered Kellie his hand, she took it, her gold band sparkling in the sunshine. They danced to the reggae music of the traditional steel players, joined by many of their guests, as the party continued long into the evening.

At the point the sun began to set, Steve and Kellie escaped the fun of the party for a short while and strolled down to the water's edge. Hand in hand, they were very much in love and as they looked out at the beautifully calm sea in front of them, Steve told Kellie he wanted to make her and their baby a personal vow. He turned her to face him and with his right hand on her tummy, he took her left hand and placed it over his heart as he promised to love, cherish and protect both her and their child, throughout their whole lifetime together, which he hoped would be infinite. As he kissed her to seal in his promise, Kellie felt a warmth of love which completely filled her heart and mind. This was indeed true love and as she kissed Steve back, she also promised herself to him until the day they both left this earth.

As the sun fell closer to the horizon, the sky turned bright orange, it looked like an Egyptian sun. Their fate was sealed. Music was playing. Family and friends were partying. Laughter and happy chatter could be heard along the beach, as the newly-wed husband and wife strolled back to re-join their guests.

Chapter 14

Karma

Two days after their wedding, Kellie and Steve were on-board a small and very old steamer ship, which was the sailing vessel that would take them along the Nile. Aptly named the *Cleopatra*, it was very much loved by its crew, as they proudly cleaned and polished its beautiful fittings, some of which were looking a little worn, having lived a long lifetime of journeys, carrying the wealthy up and down the long length of the Egyptian Nile. The old steamer had six cabins on the deck-level which were used for paying guests. Below deck were the kitchen, engine room and rooms shared by the crew, who worked in shifts to keep the steamer moving.

The friendly crew were very experienced in taking care of their foreign paying guests and had planned a sumptuous meal for their first night, having learnt from past excursions that travellers generally needed a night of simple relaxation, some local food and to meet their fellow travellers, before settling into their beautiful Egyptian themed cabins. All of which had colourful, luxurious fabrics which covered the beds, along with multitudes of cushions adorning the many seating areas.

Kellie had gasped as they'd first walked into their cabin whilst Steve, knowing her love of ancient Egypt, had glowed with pride at seeing the happiness on Kellie's face. There were no words to describe how immensely happy and impressed she was, that Steve had planned such a perfect honeymoon for them to share; this was like having their own private boat and Kellie told him there was nothing better that he could have chosen.

Steve watched as she touched the different fabrics, marvelling at the intricate embroidery on some of the older pieces and delighting in their luxurious beauty. He too was impressed with the luxurious feel of the otherwise very simple cabin. "I'm thrilled that you love it so much, Kellie. I knew as soon as I found it, that it would be just perfect for us." Kellie looked at him with shining eyes and a beaming smile; she really did love this man and told him so again. Steve preened with pride and positively glowed inside.

The two of them spent the next hour unpacking and organising themselves before moving out onto the deck. Standing by the handrail, they looked up at the relatively unpolluted night sky; it was a truly awesome sight to see the darkness filled with billions of stars. It really was the most perfect honeymoon and Kellie felt like her heart might burst with happiness. As Steve grinned first at her and then up at the stars, he was thrilled that after searching high and low, he had found this fabulous old steamer, which had pleased Kellie so much.

Dinner was served on deck, under the front canopy, where there was a single large table, laden with lots of different dishes which everyone sat around together, to meet and enjoy the company of their fellow travellers. They were a mixed bunch and each had their own fascination for Egypt's ancient history. On one side of the table were two sisters from England, Daisy and Dottie, both in their seventies and very much old school, in that they revelled at the opportunity to dress and act as if they were from the actual era of the very old steamer they were all travelling upon. Sat at the head of table and who was also in the cabin next to theirs, was Michael, a historian travelling alone, yet unexpectedly, very sharp witted. He was also full of historical Egyptian information which he happily shared with anyone who was interested enough to listen, often with an amusing story attached, which entertained his audience greatly. Kellie found herself absorbing all the details of whatever Michael shared about ancient Egypt, whilst the others laughed at his jokes. Unsure of where their new travel-mate was from, Steve and Kellie were both quietly wondering when Michael answered the question for them; he was actually Greek and having never married or had children, he was currently single. They also reckoned he must be in his late thirties or early forties. Then there was Mal and his wife Rosie, who were American, and very kind, gentle folk, emitting a fabulous warmth and honesty, which drew people to them like a magnet. It seemed like they'd had a tough life, albeit a happy one, working long and hard at their own business and raising a family along the way. Until now, when in their sixties, they were finally enjoying their time together, having been able to retire early and travel the world. Which they also admitted, had been something they could only dream of when they were much younger, what with five children to take care of, as well as their business.

Kellie and Steve very much liked all of their fellow travellers and felt very fortunate at how easily all of the different personalities seemed to blend together so well; particularly considering their different ages and backgrounds. Kellie and Steve were the youngest in the group, but they found that age didn't seem to matter, as, along with all of the others, they chattered away until late into the evening. When tiredness eventually overcame them all and they decided to head off to bed, each of them thanked their crew for such a fabulous meal and evening, before saying goodnight to their fellow travellers. Everyone was excited about the journey they were starting out on and all were keen to get going, having very much enjoyed their first evening together. It was going to be a trip of a lifetime and one to definitely remember, of that they were all certain.

The following day the crew reminded them all of the dangers of sun-stroke and suggested they would be best to keep hats on and avoid sitting in the sun for too long. Kellie knew the heat would be unbearable when they reached Aswan, which was also known as Swenett in ancient Egypt. Having read much about the small garrison town, Kellie knew it was where the armies of ancient Egypt are said to have lived; she had always wondered why they would choose to reside in a place so hot. Now experiencing Egypt's heat for herself, she imagined that the journey in and out of the many camps must have been a living hell. Steve had agreed with her, having felt the fierceness of desert heat blowing across the land towards them. But despite the heat, they were both enraptured by Egypt and its ancient history.

Kellie could hardly contain her excitement as each day passed and they visited every kind of monument, viewing artefacts that the ancient people of Egypt would have also touched, hundreds of years ago. The whole group, including Steve, were enjoying this journey into what felt like the past life, of a much more modern-day Egypt.

Michael, their very own historian, along with Kellie, had been able to share many facts and interesting stories about how Egypt was formed by the people who once lived there. Their group and the crew were equally impressed by their extensive knowledge, which improved the enjoyment of every day of their trip, as they all marvelled at how truly amazing it was that the artefacts and buildings they saw, could have survived for so long, and some with considerably less damage than you would imagine.

On the day they approached the location that was considered to have been Cleopatra's home, the Captain told them he planned to moor overnight, adding that they had special permission to explore the ruins as much as they pleased, but only whilst the daylight held and reminding them all that the night temperatures would feel considerably cooler after the heat of the day. Steve was surprised that they could actually see the ruins from the boat and as they neared the docking point, he watched Kellie, her excitement was almost tangible. Steve, knowing her interest in Cleopatra in particular, knew that this place would likely have an emotional effect on Kellie, so he was on guard to look after and protect her.

As they disembarked from the steamer and walked towards the ruins, it was Kellie's turn to be amazed, because although she had seen pictures in books, she had never imagined actually being there and able to touch the ancient walls and pillars.

The previous evening, whilst in the privacy of their cabin, Steve and Kellie had discussed taking the golden dagger ashore with them and burying it somewhere, in a place where it could not easily be found. The idea had seemed perfect, even slightly ironic, that the dagger should be returned to its original homeland by Kellie. But now, Steve was wondering if there would even be such a place, or indeed, if they would find themselves carrying the dagger back home with them, afraid that another visitor might find it.

The earth was hot under their feet, but each of them felt surprisingly glad of the break from being afloat. Knowing Steve and Kellie were on honeymoon, their fellow travellers all appreciated that the two young lovers would most probably like some time to be alone, away from their ship-mates. So, Daisy and Dottie decided to wander around with Mal and Rosie, whilst Michael excused himself and headed off alone, claiming to be anxious to explore as much as he could before they had to return to the boat.

To Kellie, the place was strangely familiar, but larger than she had imagined it would be. Remembering the many servants and guards who would have also resided there, Kellie realised that of course, the palace would have been quite sprawling to accommodate all of its resident subjects. As Kellie and Steve explored, the ruins became more and more familiar to Kellie and she was becoming more animated about every part she was seeing. It was almost as if Jocelyn was taking over her mind and wanting to show her everything.

Having climbed to the highest point and now looking out over the Nile, which stretched away as far as the eye could see, Kellie and Steve looked around. Some way in the distance, they could see the place where Jocelyn and Ibrahim the Black had first made love. They didn't know for sure that it was the actual place, but suddenly, once again, Kellie felt as if she was Jocelyn, confirming to Steve and herself that it was exactly the place.

Steve was intrigued and a little worried as he watched Kellie, for he too felt that she was being guided by a presence, one which was determined that Kellie should see every part of the palace that was so important to Jocelyn. As she guided them both to places where she had shared her life with Ibrahim, including the room in which she had birthed their stillborn child, Steve also began to sense something more. And before Kellie could say anything, Steve told her he was certain they were now walking towards the very place where Ibrahim and Jocelyn had spent their last moments together, as he lay dying from the fatal wound caused by the golden dagger in the hands of Simona. Steve couldn't explain how he knew that, he just did and as they arrived at the entrance of the room in which Ibrahim had died, so Steve took Kellie's hand and lifted her fingers to his lips. As he kissed them gently, his voice changed tone and he spoke with an accent:

"My darling, Jocelyn, however could I leave you. I loved you more than words could ever say and I wanted to live the life we planned, but that was taken from me. I have always tried to stay close to you. Know that I will always

be yours."

Kellie was surprised, not just because Steve had called her Jocelyn, but because his eyes and voice were strangely different. Something spiritual was happening to them both, which was so intense and not within their control. It captured them both in a fleeting moment in time.

As Kellie replied, her own voice changed pitch and she looked deeply into Steve's eyes, love evident, as she gazed at him.

"You were my one true love, Ibrahim, and I will always love you. I wanted us to be together forever, living by the Sea of Galilee and I couldn't bear it when I lost both you and our baby. I think of you constantly, my darling, and my heart will always be yours."

The energy around them was tangible and as they stood holding hands and staring into each other's eyes, the energy surrounding them crackled.

A shadow fell across them and out from behind a pillar stepped a familiar face, it was Michael who stood there; at least, they thought it was him, but he looked so much older and was dressed in ancient robes. His face was kindly as he looked upon these two young people and a feeling of immense love encircled them as he reached out his open hands towards them. He was asking for the golden dagger and for forgiveness of his daughter, explaining that he was Abraham, as he stood before them, his hands outstretched awaiting the dagger to be placed on them as a very young Charlotte Terry also stepped out from behind him. Looking up to him as he glanced down at her, Abraham explained that this was his beloved daughter, Simona.

Kellie placed the dagger into the palms of Abraham's hands, as Simona took it into hers and spoke: *"I know of no other way to prove my sorrow at what I did to you both."*

160

Then turning the tip of the dagger towards herself, she plunged the dagger into her own abdomen, whispering quietly, *"Forgive me."* As Abraham caught his daughter in his arms and lifted her up, with tears in his eyes, he explained that Simona had wanted to right the wrong she had done and that she had now surrendered her spirit, so that Kellie and Steve, and their baby Mary, could live a long and happy life together, in their new *House of Galilee*.

As he turned to walk away, with his daughter slumped in his arms, Abraham told them that this was right and that they were not to feel badly. He explained that now Simona had relieved her own pain, she could now rest in peace, having forgiven herself. Father and daughter could now become part of the same spiritual energy that had brought them both to earth together, all those years ago. And with that last breath, the image of Abraham and Simona faded, joining the universal life force energy that created our world.

Kellie and Steve were in shock: how could they tell anyone what had just happened and how would they explain what had happened to Michael? Making their way back to the steamer, they held onto each other tightly, unable to speak. As they re-joined their group, the Captain told them that Michael had previously informed him that he would be disembarking and not re-joining the cruise, but to send each of them his very best wishes for a happy future.

Steve and Kellie looked at each other, both feeling compassion for Simona and Abraham and relief at no longer needing to explain about Michael. Yet in equal measures, they also felt eternal love and hope for a happy life together and the joy their new baby daughter would bring; a girl they would call Mary and who would be born in their *House of Galilee*.

Lightning Source UK Ltd.
Milton Keynes UK
UKHW042232030220
357983UK00016B/36

9 781787 195783